Dear Kelly,

Another day dawns and I am still here in this miserable cell. But then you come, if only in my dreams…

You come after sunset. Tonight you are sixteen, and when you smile, I suddenly realise you are wearing your prom dress. You are so beautiful, my heart nearly stops beating.

You lean forward to kiss me, and I can feel your soft lips, smell your perfume. You take me with you, back in time, and for a while I am out of here. I sit with you in my sports car, wearing my tuxedo, and we kiss.

You are still so young, and I still don't know any better. I can't stop myself.

I love you.

Love, T.

Available in January 2004 from Silhouette Sensation

Letters to Kelly
by Suzanne Brockmann

In the Line of Fire
by Beverly Bird
(The Country Club)

Alias Smith and Jones
by Kylie Brant
(The Tremaine Tradition)

Wilder Days
by Linda Winstead Jones

Smoke and Mirrors
by Jenna Mills

On Thin Ice
by Debra Lee Brown

Letters to Kelly

SUZANNE BROCKMANN

SILHOUETTE®
SENSATION™

First published in Great Britain 2004
Silhouette Books, Eton House, 18-24 Paradise Road,
Richmond, Surrey TW9 1SR

© Suzanne Brockmann 2003

ISBN 0 373 27283 9

18-0104

Printed and bound in Spain
by Litografía Rosés S.A., Barcelona

SUZANNE BROCKMANN

lives just west of Boston in a house always filled with her friends—actors and musicians and storytellers and artists and teachers. When not writing award-winning romances about US Navy SEALs, among others, she sings in an a capella group called Serious Fun, manages the professional acting careers of her two children, volunteers at the Appalachian Benefit Coffeehouse and always answers letters from readers. Send an SAE with return postage to PO Box 5092, Wayland, MA 01778, USA.

To my wonderful mother, Lee Brockmann,
who's been waiting a long time for this one.

Chapter 1

Kelly O'Brien lugged her heavy canvas bag of books into the back door of the university newspaper office. The spring day was hot, and a trickle of sweat dripped uncomfortably down her back.

She heaved the book bag onto her desk with a crash, and pushed back the damp strands of long, dark hair that had escaped from her bun. With a sigh, she peeled off her jacket and undid the top buttons of her sleeveless blouse, shaking the neckline slightly to let fresh air circulate against her overheated body.

"Psst."

Kelly looked up to see Marcy Reynolds, the school newspaper's student photographer, hissing at her. Marcy's brown eyes were lit with excitement, her pixielike face alive with curiosity.

"There's some guy sitting in the front office, waiting for you," Marcy said, handing Kelly several pink phone message slips. "No. Correction—this is not just some guy. This is a Man, with a capital *M*. And quite possibly *the* most gorgeous man who has ever crossed the threshold of this humble establishment.''

Kelly smiled. ''Oh, come on—''

''I'm serious,'' the younger woman said. As she shook her head, her large hoop earrings bumped the sides of her face. ''We're talking major heart-attack material. *Very* tall, blond, green eyes—he's a dead ringer for Mel Gibson's cuter, younger brother. The man is a walking blue jeans ad, Kelly. His legs are about a mile long, and those buns…''

Kelly laughed in disbelief. ''He sounds too good to be true,'' she said.

''He looks like one of the heroes from those romance novels you're writing. He's been sitting there for forty-five minutes,'' Marcy complained, running her fingers through her short black hair, ''totally blowing my concentration.''

''Is he a student?''

''He's too old,'' Marcy said. ''I mean, unless he took some time off from school, but not only a few years, like you. Like serious time, maybe ten years. I'd say he's maybe thirty. He's got those sexy little crinkly laugh lines around his eyes. Check him out— he's a total babe.''

''Maybe he's a professor,'' Kelly said. ''Did he say what he wants?''

''*You're* what he wants.'' Marcy smirked. ''That's all he said. I told him I didn't know when you'd be back—that you could be gone for hours. But he just said he'd wait. He said something about waiting seven years, and that another few hours wouldn't kill him. Have you been keeping this man on the shelf for *seven years?*''

"Seven years ago I was only sixteen," Kelly said. She moved to the glass partition that separated the front office from the back. The blinds were down and shut, and she moved one aluminum slat a fraction of an inch and peeked out.

Her heart stopped.

T. Jackson Winchester the Second.

It couldn't be.

But it was.

He was the only person in the outer office and he sat by the door, one ankle resting on one knee, leaning casually back in his chair, as comfortable as if he were in his own living room. He wore a royal-blue polo shirt with both buttons open, revealing his sun-kissed neck and chest. His shirt was tucked into a pair of faded blue jeans that hugged his muscular thighs. On his feet he wore Docksiders but no socks. His ankles were strong and tan.

He was reading the latest copy of the school newspaper, and his eyes were down, hidden by long, dark lashes. Kelly didn't need to see his eyes to know they were a remarkable mix of colors, with a ring of yellow gold, like solar flares, that surrounded his pupils. The edges of his irises were brilliant green. And sandwiched between the green and the gold was the ocean. Like the ocean, his eyes changed. They could be stormy gray, or dark blue-black, or even a deep, mysterious shade of green. She could remember looking into his eyes, into a warm swirl of colored fire, his lips curving up into a smile as he bent to kiss her—

Kelly shook her head, pushing the thought away. She looked at him again, closely this time, searching for signs of age, signs of change.

He was wearing his golden hair longer than she'd

ever seen him wear it before, hanging down several inches over his collar, thick and wavy and blond and soft. His face had a few more lines, but if anything, he was even more handsome than ever.

He looked really good.

But he'd always looked good. He'd looked good when she'd first met him, and he'd been hung over at the time. She could still remember that morning as if it were yesterday, not eleven years ago....

Twelve-year-old Kelly had opened the door quietly, carefully, then slipped into the darkened guest bedroom. She had heard the clock ticking, and the sound of slow, steady breathing.

Her brother Kevin's mysterious college roommate was lying sprawled out on the bed, long legs escaping from beneath the covers that were twisted around him. One arm was flung above his head, the other lay across his bare chest.

His name was T. Jackson Winchester the Second. Kevin had called from school to tell her parents about the freshman dorm and about his roommate. Kelly had been particularly impressed by the length of his roommate's name. Kevin had told their father that T. Jackson was from Cape Cod, and he drove a Triumph Spitfire.

What did the T. stand for? Kelly had wondered. And what color was the Spitfire?

Red. She'd made a point of looking out onto the driveway first thing when she woke up. The Spitfire was shiny and red, with a black convertible top.

Kelly stepped closer to T. Jackson Winchester the Second, to get a better look at him in the dimness of the room, to see what a rich college roommate looked like.

He had an awful lot of muscles. Kevin was eighteen, and he had lots of muscles, too, but Kelly had never given his muscles a second glance. He was her brother, sometimes a pain in the neck, sometimes a creep, but mostly fun.

This guy, however, was not her brother.

She swallowed hard, looking down at his messy blond hair and his handsome face. He was definitely a ten. A living ten. Kelly had seen some tens before on television or in the movies. But before this, she'd never met one face-to-face.

His face was perfectly shaped with a long, straight nose and a strong jawline. His eyebrows were two slightly curved light brown lines above the thick eyelashes that lay against the smooth, tanned skin of his cheeks. His lips were neither too thin nor too thick, and nicely shaped. Even in sleep, they tended to curve upward, as if a smile was his natural expression.

Kelly leaned even closer, wondering what color his eyes were, then wondering with a flash of giddiness what color his underpants were. She clapped her hand over her mouth to keep a laugh from escaping and backed away from the bed.

She'd come into this room with a purpose, and although checking out T. Jackson Winchester the Second was interesting, that wasn't why she'd crept in. She moved quietly to the closet. The door was closed, and she silently slid it open, carefully stopping it before it bumped the frame.

Oh, man, her mother had moved her rock-collecting gear up onto the top shelf.

Kelly was tall for her age, but she still couldn't reach the backpack that sat on the top shelf in the closet. Not without climbing on a chair.

The only chair in the room was clear over on the other side, below the shaded window. Stealthily Kelly moved toward it. T. Jackson Winchester the Second had draped his jeans and shirt over the back of the chair last night before he climbed into bed.

Staggered into bed was more like it. Kelly wrinkled her nose as she smelled the odor of stale cigarette smoke and beer that seemed to cling to T. Jackson's clothes. He and Kevin had been to some kind of wild party last night. Some *illegal* wild party.

The drinking age in Massachusetts was twenty-one. She'd heard her father arguing with Kevin about that. Her brother insisted if he was old enough to register for the draft, then he was old enough to drink. Her father had countered by saying if he was old enough to drink, then he was also old enough to always pick a designated driver. Dad had added that if he ever caught Kevin drinking and driving, no matter *how* old he was, he'd be grounded for ten years.

From the looks of ol' T. Jackson Winchester the Second, Kevin had probably been last night's designated driver.

Kelly dropped the clothes onto the floor and wrestled the heavy chair toward the closet. But she didn't see the big high-top sneakers that were lying in the way, and she tripped, hitting the floor with a crash and a yelp as the chair fell on top of her.

Before she could move, the chair was pulled away. "Are you all right?" T. Jackson Winchester the Second said raspily, frowning down at her with concern.

Red.

He was wearing boxer shorts and they were red. As Kelly stared way, way up at him, she wondered whether it was a coincidence, or if he always matched his underwear to the color of the car he was driving.

"Did you hurt yourself, kid?" he asked, after clearing his throat noisily and swallowing hard as if his mouth was dry. He reached out a hand to help her to her feet.

His hand was big and warm, with long, strong fingers and carefully manicured nails. Kelly let go quickly, afraid to be caught clinging foolishly, grinning at him like an idiot.

"I'll live," she said. She was going to get some big bruise on her leg where the chair had hit her, but she wasn't about to tell T. Jackson Winchester the Second about it.

As she watched, he crossed to the bedside table and drained a glass of water that was sitting there.

"Ugh," she said, wrinkling her nose. "Isn't that warm?"

He glanced at her, putting the empty glass back down. "It's wet," he said. "That's all that matters." He ran his hands over his face and looked longingly at the bed. "What time is it?" he asked.

"About quarter to nine," she told him. "How tall *are* you exactly?"

He sat down on the bed, resting his forehead in his hands. "Exactly?" he asked, looking up at her through his fingers, a glint of amusement in his eyes. "Six foot four and one quarter inches."

"That's tall." Kelly nodded. "I'm Kelly O'Brien," she added.

T. Jackson Winchester the Second straightened up the best that he could and held out his hand. "Pleased to meet you, Kelly O'Brien," he said, somehow managing to smile. "I'm Jax, Kevin's roommate."

Kelly took his hand, shaking it firmly. "T. Jackson Winchester the Second," she said. "I know."

Green eyes. He had green eyes, rimmed with red. "Christmas in October," she said, and grinned.

Somehow he understood that she was talking about his eyes, and he smiled ruefully. "I look bad, huh?"

Kelly nodded. "You look like hell."

He laughed with a flash of straight, white teeth. Forget ten. He was clearly an eleven.

"Sorry I woke you up," she said. "I was trying to get my backpack down from the closet shelf."

"This isn't your room, is it?" he said, frowning slightly as he looked around at the impersonal guest room, at the blandly patterned bedspread, the flower print on the curtains, the beige carpeting.

"Nah," Kelly said. "I just use the closet because I'm overflowing my own. What does the T. stand for?"

He looked at her blankly. "The…what?"

"In your name," she said patiently. "You know. *T. Jackson*…? And you call yourself Jacks? Like the game? Or is it a plural, as if there's two of you?"

He laughed again, then winced as if his head hurt. "No, there's only one of me. It's spelled *J-A-X*," he said. "It's a nickname."

"And the *T.*?"

"Tyrone," he said with a grimace.

"Ew."

"Yeah. That's why I keep it an initial."

"Tyrone," Kelly said slowly. "Ty. Well, it's not really *that* bad. But 'Jax' is pretty weird. Why don't you go for the entire initial thing? You know, call yourself T.J.?"

He stood slowly, steadying himself on one of the bedposts. "It's taken," he said. "My father is T.J."

"The First."

"You got it."

"Doesn't that actually make you *Junior?*" Kelly asked critically. "I mean, this 'the Second' stuff is kind of pompous, don't you think?"

Jax grinned, crossing toward the closet. "If you ask me, the whole Winchester existence is kind of pompous."

"I'll call you T.," she decided. "I like that better than Jax."

He turned toward her. "Look, if I get your backpack down for you, will you let me go back to sleep?"

She smiled. "Promise to take me for a ride later in your Spitfire and you've got a deal."

Jackson smiled back at her, his warm green eyes taking her in from the top of her boyishly short hair, to her faded turtleneck with the too-short sleeves and her skinny wrists sticking out, to her ragged jeans and right down to her worn-out cowboy boots. He stared at her for so long that Kelly wiped her nose, wondering if maybe it was running.

But his smile slowly faded, and he frowned down at himself, as if suddenly aware he was half-naked. "I probably shouldn't be standing here in my underwear, talking to you like this."

"I've seen Kevin in his underwear more times than I can count," Kelly scoffed. "It's no big deal."

"Yeah, but Kev's your brother," Jax said. "I'm not."

Looking at him, Kelly was glad that he wasn't. No one should have a brother who looked as good as T. Jackson Winchester the Second.

"Something tells me that your father wouldn't approve." Jax grinned. "And I don't want to be forced into any kind of a shotgun wedding, no matter how pretty you are."

Kelly felt herself blush. "Don't be a jerk," she warned him. "I know exactly what I look like." She was a skinny beanpole with a faintly feminine face. If she stretched her imagination, she could use the word *pretty* to describe her eyes. But only her eyes.

"Is this what you need?" Jax asked, pointing to a blue backpack in the closet.

She nodded.

He swung it down, but it was heavier than he thought, and he had to lunge to keep from dropping it. "God," he said, "what have you got in here? Rocks?"

Kelly smiled, taking the knapsack from him, her muscles straining as she slipped it over her shoulder. "Yeah. It's my rock collection."

Jax looked surprised, then he laughed. "You're into geology, huh?" he said. "Will you show me your collection later?"

"Yeah." Kelly nodded, smiling at him again. She turned to go, but looked back at him, her hand on the doorknob. "T. Jackson Winchester the Second," she said, "you're not a dweeb. I like you. My brother's lucky he got you for a roommate."

He'd laughed again as Kelly had gone out the door. "I like you, too, Kelly," she'd heard him say. "And *I'm* lucky that I got a roommate with a sister like you. See you later...."

Kelly now lowered the slat on the blinds, and looking down, realized that she had scrunched the phone message slips she'd been holding into a tight wad of paper.

"Do you know him?" Marcy's words finally penetrated.

"Yeah," Kelly said slowly.

"Who *is* he?"

Good question. Was he a childhood friend? A friend of the family? An almost-lover? Kelly went for the obvious. "He was my brother's college roommate," she said. She turned to Marcy suddenly. "Do me a favor and tell him that I just called and told you that I wasn't coming back in today."

Marcy was looking at her as if she had finally lost her mind. "And just which telephone line is it that you supposedly called on?" she said. "The one that rings silently?"

"Tell him—" Kelly was grabbing wildly now. "Tell him *you* called me."

Marcy folded her arms across her chest, the bangles and bracelets she wore on her wrists jangling. "I talked to the man for maybe five minutes when he first came in, but it was long enough for me to know he's no idiot," she said. "Now, if I go out there making excuses for you, girl, he's gonna realize that you took one look at him and ran away. And a man like that one—" she gestured toward the door to the outer office "—usually does only one thing when he's being run away from." She paused for emphasis. "He gives chase. So unless you want this guy following you all over town—and if you do, that's fine, because *I* sure wouldn't mind—you better take a nice deep breath, and go and talk to him."

Marcy was right. She was absolutely right.

Kelly walked to the door and, following her friend's advice, took a deep breath. She glanced back at Marcy for an extra dose of strength, then turned the doorknob.

Chapter 2

Jax stared at the college newspaper without reading it. He tried thinking about the book he was writing, tried to plan the next scene, but he couldn't even keep his mind on that. He was nervous. What if Kelly didn't show up?

What if she did?

Relax, he ordered himself. It's just Kelly.

Just Kelly.

It had been seven years since the night of her junior prom.

God, his life could have been so different if he hadn't been so stupid. But he made a mistake, and here he was, seven years later, no closer to getting what he wanted.

Seven long, wasted years...

Jax wished he could go back in time, do it all over again. Well, not *all*. He'd skip the trip to Central America, thank you very much. Yeah, he'd pass on *that* ten-day news-gathering expedition that had turned into a twenty-month nightmare—

He took a deep breath. He had dreamed about Central America last night for the first time in a long time. He'd dreamed he was back in the prison and—

But he didn't want to think about *that,* either. He was better off just worrying about Kelly. Seven years was a long time. She must have changed. Lord knows he had.

But since yesterday, when Kevin had called and filled him in on the latest O'Brien family news, Jax felt twenty-two years old again. All of his optimism and hope flooded back, as if it had never faded and disappeared.

Kelly was back in Boston, Kevin had told him, finishing her college degree. She had gotten a divorce.

Even as Jax had talked to Kevin on the phone, even as he had made regretful noises over Kelly's failed marriage, he'd done a silent victory dance in his living room.

Kelly was single. She was single and she wasn't too young anymore. Jax smiled as he stared sightlessly down at the newspaper he was holding.

He could still see her, the way she had looked when he'd first met her. She'd been only twelve years old, no more than a child, but her dark blue eyes held the maturity and wisdom of a woman twice her age. With her dry wit, she was clearly intelligent, but it was her steady self-confidence that made him adore her—not to mention the promise of incredible beauty he could see in her face.

And as he found himself spending more and more time with the O'Briens, his feelings for Kelly grew as she did.

And though the O'Briens didn't have a fraction of the money that his parents had, in Jax's mind, the Winchesters were the losers.

Nolan and Lori O'Brien had been married twenty years when Jax had first met them, but they still loved each other, and maybe even more important, they still genuinely *liked* each other. And they truly loved their children. They couldn't give Kevin and Kelly expensive gifts, they couldn't even afford to send Kevin to Boston College without the help from his scholarship, but there was certainly no lack of love in that family.

And the O'Briens had opened their arms to Jax, encircling him with all the love and laughter and music that always seemed to shake the foundation of their little house.

Jax had even spent one entire summer living with them—along with Lori's recently divorced sister, Christa, and her three children. It had been a magnificent summer, the best he could remember. The house had been so crowded that he and Kevin had to sleep on bedrolls out on the screened-in porch. When it rained, they sought refuge on the floor in Kelly's room.

Kelly had been fourteen that summer, her long legs and arms beginning to change from skinny to willowy. She had grown her dark hair long, and she wore it in a single braid down her back.

She still called Jax "T." or sometimes even Tyrone. She was the only person in the universe he would let get away with that.

He hadn't gone out on a single date that entire summer, spending most of his evenings playing Risk or Monopoly with the ready crowd of O'Briens and relatives. But if anyone had accused him at that time of having anything other than a friendly, platonic love for Kelly, he would have furiously denied it. He was a twenty-year-old man, for crying out loud. Kelly was just a kid.

It wasn't until two years later, until the night of Kelly's junior prom—

"T. Jackson Winchester the Second." Kelly's husky voice interrupted his thoughts, and he looked up from the newspaper into a pair of familiar blue eyes.

Kelly.

Jax forced himself to move slowly. He slowly folded the newspaper and put it on the table beside him. He slowly got to his feet and smiled down at her.

God, she had become even more beautiful than she'd been the last time he'd seen her, four years ago at Kevin's wedding.

Her eyes were a deep, dark shade of blue and exquisitely shaped. Her skin was smooth and fair, contrasting with her rich brown hair and her long, dark eyelashes. Her face was elegantly heart-shaped, with a small, strong chin and a perfect nose. She was gorgeous. She'd always been remarkably pretty as a girl, but as a woman, she was breathtaking.

"Kelly." It came out little more than a whisper.

"How are you?" she asked. "What are you doing here?"

Jax cleared his throat and ran his hand through his hair. "I'm in town on business," he said. It wasn't entirely a lie. True, the business could just as easily have been done over the telephone, but... "I thought I'd come and ask you to have dinner with me. I didn't realize you were back in Boston until I spoke to Kevin yesterday."

As Kelly looked up into his eyes, she was struck by how little T. Jackson had changed. He was still the same poised, confident, charismatic and utterly charming man he'd always been. There was no situation he would be uncomfortable in, nothing that could rattle him—no, that wasn't entirely true. She *had* seen him severely shaken up, even out of control. But only once. It had been the night of her junior prom.

"So how about it?" Jax smiled as he returned her steady gaze. "Will you have dinner with me?"

It was Plan "A." He would take her to dinner tonight, and again tomorrow night, and by Wednesday she'd remember how good they were together. She'd realize that their friendship had survived all those years they'd spent apart. And then he'd kiss her goodnight, let her know he wanted them to be more than friends. By the end of the week, he'd ask her to marry him. It was fast, but it couldn't exactly be called a whirlwind courtship considering that he'd really started courting her back before he even realized it, back when she was only twelve years old.

It was a plan that would work. He knew it would work.

But he could see wariness in Kelly's eyes. "I don't think so," she said, shaking her head no.

She had turned him down. He hadn't figured *that* possibility when he was making his plan. This was one scenario he had never considered. Despite the heat of the day, Jax felt a sudden chill. Was he too late again? Was he destined to go through life with the woman he wanted always one step out of his reach?

"Are you seeing someone?" he asked.

Kelly looked away. "No."

Jax fought to hide his relief from showing on his face.

"It's just…not necessary for you to take me out to dinner," she said, pushing a wisp of hair from her face.

Jax laughed then. "Says who?"

She sighed and crossed her arms in front of her. "Look, I know Kevin called you because he's worried about me. I've been…a little down. Give me a break, I just got a divorce. I'm allowed to be depressed. I was brought up believing that marriage was permanent, but Brad and I didn't even manage to hold it together for three years."

As Jax watched, she looked down at the floor. Her unhappiness was clearly evident in her eyes, in the tightness of her mouth. Good grief, another variable he hadn't considered. "Do you still love him?" he asked softly.

She glanced up at Jax, and her eyes were filled with tears. "You know what the really stupid thing is, T.?"

He shook his head silently, wishing that he could take her in his arms. But he was held back by all those years of purposely not touching her. During the five years that he'd been in college, the five years that they'd been such good friends, he'd always been very careful not to touch her. Not casually, not at all. It was as if he subconsciously knew there could only be one kind of physical relationship between them, and that there would be nothing casual about it.

"I don't think I ever loved him," she said.

One of Kelly's tears ran down her cheek, and Jax couldn't stop from reaching out to brush it away. She took a step back, as if the contact had burned her.

"Don't."

"Sorry," he said quickly. "I'm sorry."

Kelly wiped her face with the back of her hand, blinking away the rest of her tears. T. was looking at her with such anxiety in his eyes, it almost made her laugh. T. Jackson anxious? She wouldn't have believed it possible. She managed a shaky smile.

"You think I'm a real basket case, right?" she asked.

"I think you could use a friend," he said quietly.

"Yeah," she said, hugging her crossed arms close to her body, as if she were cold, as if it weren't more than eighty degrees in the newspaper office. "I could. But not you, Tyrone. Not this time."

"Why not?"

But it was as if she hadn't heard him. "Just tell Kevin I'm okay. I'm going to be fine. But I'll be fine a lot sooner without you hanging around, doing my brother a favor."

Jax choked on the air he was breathing. "I'm *not* here to do Kevin a favor," he said.

"Yeah, well, it wouldn't be the first time," Kelly said, "would it?"

Jax laughed, but then stopped as the meaning of what she was saying washed over him like a cold bucket of water. "Oh, God," he said. "You believed what Kevin said that morning after the prom?"

"Of course I believed him," Kelly said. "You didn't deny it." She turned toward the door to the back office. "I've got to go. Thanks for dropping by."

"Kelly, wait—"

But she was gone.

Jax stood there for a long time even though he knew she'd gone out the back door, even though he knew that she wasn't coming back.

So much for Plan "A."

* * *

Jax set his laptop computer on the dining table in his hotel suite, attached the power cord and plugged it into the wall. He hit the On switch and the computer wheezed to life.

He pulled his spiral notebook and his collection of computer disks out of his briefcase and found the one labeled Jared.

This book was an historical, with most of the action taking place during the Civil War era. He'd written a number of Civil War books before, so the research he'd had to do for this one had been minimal. This book was going to be fast and easy, especially since the story was one he was extremely familiar with.

He put the disk into the computer's drive and called up the job. After less than a week of work, he was already up to page 163, and he'd just finished writing the explosive, pivotal fight scene between Jared, the hero, and Edmund, the heroine's brother.

He quickly skimmed the last few pages that he'd written, but it was all still fresh in his memory, so he went right to work, starting the next scene.

With bleakness in his eyes, Jared stared at the heavy wrought-iron gates that separated him from Sinclair Manor. The gates had been shut when night had fallen, just as they had been every night. In the morning the servants would come out, unlock them, and throw them open wide.

As Jared stood in the darkness, his gaze moving up to the brightly lit house on the hill, he knew without a doubt that, day or night, he was no longer welcome there. Those gates had been closed to him forever.

Jax stopped writing to take a sip from a can of soda. Now what? Now Jared had to get over that fence.

But Carrie was in there, and welcome or not, Jared meant to have her. With an effortless leap, he climbed up, up and over the sharp spikes that decked the top of the tall fence, letting himself drop lightly to the ground on the other side.

He'd made a promise to Carrie. It was a promise he intended to keep.

Keeping to the trees, moving quietly, the way he'd learned as a young boy in the wilds of Kentucky, he approached the manor house. He moved with purpose, his mouth set in a grim line of determination, making his dark good looks seem almost savage, making it seem as if more than just a quarter of the blood that ran through his veins was Indian.

His gaze quickly found Carrie's bedroom window—

"Whoa, wait a minute," Jax muttered as he stopped writing. "Where do you think *you're* going?"

In his mind he could see Jared turning to stare at him, arms crossed, eyebrow raised, impatience clearly written on the character's handsome face. "I'm going to see Carrie."

"Nuh-uh-uh," Jax chided gently. "According to my outline, you're supposed to meet her in the gazebo."

"Right," Jared said with exasperation. "Only, she doesn't show, her brother Edmund does, and he beats the crap out of me again, because I'm too noble to raise a hand against him on account of the fact that he used to be my best friend. In reality, I could whip him with one hand behind my back. I'm getting tired of this, and so will all your readers.'' He glanced up at Carrie's window again. ''It's time for some sex.''

Jax crossed his arms, leaning back with a sigh. His heroes were all alike. They all wanted immediate, instant gratification. They all loved the heroines desperately, and couldn't understand why Jax made them go through all sorts of contortions before being allowed to live happily ever after.

Of course, the *New York Times* bestseller list meant nothing to them.

''I love Carrie,'' Jared was arguing right now. ''And she loves me. I know it—she told me in that last scene you wrote. Face it, Jax, there's no way on earth I'd get on a boat for Europe and leave her behind. It's entirely out of character.''

''No, it's not,'' Jax said quietly. ''Not if you thought it was the best thing for Carrie.''

Jared sighed, shaking his head slowly. ''Carrie? Or Kelly? This is fiction, Jax. Don't get it confused with the things that went wrong in *your* life.''

''If things don't go wrong, there's no story,'' Jax pointed out. ''You want to climb up into Carrie's room and make love to her, right?''

Jared nodded.

''And you plan to sneak her out of the house, and take her with you to Europe.''

Jared nodded again, his eyes drawn once again to that dimly lit window on the second floor of the house.

''What are you going to do for money?'' Jax asked.

"Carrie is used to living a certain lifestyle. Have you thought about that?"

Jared shrugged. "I know she loves me more than money," he said with an easy smile. "As long as we're together, she'll be happy."

"You're too perfect," Jax said in disgust. "I've got to give you some insecurities, or some dark family secret."

"Oh, please, not the dark family secret thing," Jared groaned. "I'm already one-quarter Native American and dirt poor to boot. Isn't that scandalous enough?"

"Obviously not," Jax muttered. "I'd like this book to have more than 175 pages, if you don't mind."

"You want more pages?" Jared asked, his face brightening. "I've got a good idea. How about this— a hundred-page love scene? Just me and Carrie, and a hundred pages of bliss?"

Jax laughed out loud. "My, oh my, a little horny today, aren't we?"

Jared's eyes were glued to Carrie's window. "One hundred and sixty-three pages, and I've been trying to get my hands on Carrie since page one," he said. "Two different times you bring me right to the brink of ecstasy, only to snatch her away from me at the last minute. I'm dying here, Jax. Give me a break."

Jackson smiled suddenly. "All right," he said. "Go for it. Climb that trellis."

His hard gaze quickly found Carrie's bedroom window, and in a matter of moments, he was scaling the side of the house, climbing the trellis, unmindful of the thorns from the roses that scratched his hands.

Jared stopped climbing, and glared back at Jax. "You could have chosen ivy, but you had to use roses with thorns, didn't you? Man, you never give me a break."

"Roses are romantic," Jax said. "Besides, you're unmindful of them."

The window was open, and Jared quickly pushed it wider and slipped inside. He knew as soon as his feet touched her bedroom floor that something was wrong. With his heart pounding, Jared stared at the carefully stripped bed, at the empty vanity top, the barren bookshelf. Where were all of Carrie's things, all of her clutter? He strode to the wardrobe, swinging the doors open.

Empty.

All of her clothes were gone.

"Looking for something?" Edmund Sinclair's taunting voice made Jared whirl around. Carrie's brother was standing in the doorway, watching him, a sneer on his aristocratic face. "Or some-*one?*"

"Where is she?" Jared's voice was harsh.

"She's gone," Edmund said. "My father thought it best if she went to visit some relatives for a while. Funny, I can't recall whether she went to Vermont or Connecticut. Or maybe it was Maine."

Jared spun to glare at Jax. "You son of a bitch," he spat. Two large strides brought him toward Edmund, and he hauled off and punched his former friend in the face. Without another word, Jared disappeared out the window.

Jax grinned and kept writing. Yeah, it was time for Edmund to get knocked down. He'd keep that in.

Jax parked his sports car on the street outside of Kelly's apartment. Looking up, he could see the lights on in her windows. He got out of the car, grabbing the handles of the bag that held the food he'd picked up at the Chinese restaurant down the street.

If Kelly wouldn't come to dinner, dinner would come to Kelly.

She lived on the second floor of a three-family house on a quiet residential street in the Boston suburbs. Jax climbed onto the front porch and pushed the middle of three doorbells.

The evening was warm, and Jax sat back on the porch railing, watching a couple kids ride their bicycles around and around in a driveway across the street. But then the porch light came on, the door creaked open and Kelly was standing behind the screen, looking out at him.

She was wearing cut-off jeans and a ratty T-shirt, and her hair was loose around her shoulders, cascading down her back in a long, dark sheet.

He smiled at her, and she returned the smile rather ruefully, pushing open the screen door to come out onto the porch. Her feet were bare, and Jax let his eyes travel up the long lengths of her legs, feeling a still somewhat odd surge of desire. But it shouldn't be odd, he told himself. She wasn't a child anymore. She was a beautiful woman.

He could still remember the first moment he'd realized his feelings for Kevin's little sister weren't brotherly any longer. It hadn't taken him much time to shake off the feelings of oddness *that* night.

She sat down on the top step, hugging her knees in to her chest and looking up at him. "Now, why am I not surprised to see you?"

"You were expecting me?" he said with a quirk of one eyebrow. "I'm honored that you dressed for the occasion."

"Tell me you don't wish you had shorts on," Kelly said.

"You win." He smiled, just looking at her. Her dark hair was so long. He wanted to touch it, run his fingers through its silkiness, but instead he gripped the railing. "How many years did it take you to grow your hair that long?"

She swept her hair off her neck, twisting it and pulling it in front of her and frowned down at the ends. "I'm going to get it cut. I haven't done more than trim it in almost four years. I'm thinking of going radically short for the summer."

"Radically?" he asked. "You mean, like Vin Diesel?"

Kelly laughed, and Jax was momentarily transported back in time seven years, to the night of her junior prom, to the night he'd danced with her in his arms, holding her for the very first time. It seemed as if they'd spent the entire evening laughing. *Almost* the entire evening…

"That's maybe a little *too* radical," she said. "But I am thinking of getting it buzzed in the back."

She pushed her hair up as if to demonstrate just how short she wanted it cut, and Jax's eyes were drawn to her slender neck. He liked her long hair the way it was, but she would look unbelievably sexy with it short. Her hair would curl slightly around her ears, frame her beautiful face and accentuate her long, graceful neck.

"I think it would look great."

"You do?" She looked up at him, surprise in her voice.

"Yeah."

She stood. "I've got to get back to work," she said, edging toward the door.

Jax was confused. They'd been having a normal conversation, everything was very comfortable and... He was coming on too strong, he realized suddenly. He'd been distracted, thinking about how much he wanted to kiss her neck, and he'd started mentally undressing her. She knew what he was thinking from the look on his face, and now she was running away again.

He looked down at the uneven floorboards of the porch. It was the only way he could hide the desire he knew was in his eyes. "I brought over Chinese food," he said.

She shook her head no. "Thanks, but I already ate," she said. "Good night, T."

"Kelly, don't shut me out."

His quiet words made her slowly turn around to face him. "Jackson, I can't handle seeing you right now. I need some time. I need my life to be simple for a while. And face it, our relationship has never been simple."

"We can make it simple." His voice sounded calm, matter-of-fact, betraying none of his desperation.

He took a step toward her, and Kelly took a step back, panic flaring in her stomach. If he touched her, she wasn't sure she could resist him. It was bad enough seeing him, talking to him. It was frightening the way her memories of the way she used to feel for him could consume her. It was almost as if they weren't memories at all.

But there was no way she could still be in love with him, not after seven years. No way.

"I have to get back to work," she said again. "I'm sorry."

She went into the house, closing the door tightly behind her. She leaned against it for a moment before climbing up the stairs to her apartment.

Dear Kelly,
Still no word from the American consulate.

The thought of serving ten years in this hell-hole scares me to death. It's unbelievable that this farce could have come this far. I've been framed. It's as clear as the daylight that I know is shining outside, despite the fact that it barely penetrates the thick walls of this stinking cell. I'm being punished for failing to cooperate with this country's current government, failing to reveal the location of the rebel forces, failing to reveal the names of the people who led me to my meeting with the rebel leader.

What's really ridiculous is that I don't approve of many of the rebels' methods in their fight for freedom. But if I betrayed them, it would mean the death of many people, most of them women and children.

So I sit here. Wherever the hell "here" is. Somewhere in Central America. I might as well be on the moon, a million miles away from the land of the free and the home of the brave, a million miles away from your sweet smile, writing letters to you in my mind, letters that have

no hope of reaching you until I am free to deliver
them myself.

With luck, that will be soon. Your eighteenth
birthday is coming, and I intend to be there.

I love you.

Love, T.

Kelly sat at her computer, staring at the empty
screen.

Well, it wasn't quite empty. It said "Chapter Ten"
about a quarter of the way down, and there were two
carriage return symbols after that, along with a tab
symbol. The cursor flashed five spaces in, ready to
start the first paragraph.

But all she could think about was T. Jackson Winchester the Second, and the best and worst night she'd
ever had in her life. It was the best because it had
been an amazing Cinderella-like fantasy, with T. Jackson playing the part of Prince Charming. And it was
the worst, because after it was over, after all the dust
had settled, he had walked out of her life for good,
and her world turned into a pumpkin.

Until now.

Seven years later.

Kelly closed her eyes, remembering that May night.
Prom night. It had been a night like this one, hot and
humid, more like summer than spring.

That afternoon, she'd modeled her prom dress for
Kevin and T. Jackson. Kevin had just finished his first
year of law school, and T. had finally graduated from
college, having had a year off between his sophomore
and junior years. T. was hanging out with the
O'Briens, kicking back for a few weeks, taking a va-

cation before facing the realities of the working world....

"Tonight I'm going to wear my hair up," she'd said to them, twirling around the living room to show off the sweeping skirt of her long gown.

"Sweet Lord," Kevin said, staring at her. "When did *you* turn into a girl?"

She made a face at him. "Try opening your eyes sometimes, dweeb. I've been a girl for sixteen years."

She risked a glance at T. He was looking at her, a small, funny smile on his face. She smiled back at him, her heart doing a fast somersault. *He* knew that she was a girl.

"Sure could've fooled me." Kevin grinned. "I thought when you said you were going to get dressed up for the prom, you meant you'd wear your jeans without the holes in the knees and a new pair of cowboy boots."

"Ha ha," Kelly said.

"Just please don't tell me Mom bought that dress with the grocery money." Kevin made a face. "You look great, Kel, but I don't think a prom dress is worth having to eat hot dogs for the rest of the summer."

"This dress used to be Grandma's. It didn't cost a cent. Your stomach is safe."

The gown was outrageously retro, right out of the late 1930s, and it fit Kelly as if it had been made for her from some kind of shimmery, slippery cornflower-blue fabric that matched her eyes.

Kelly turned to find T. still watching her long after Kevin had gone into the kitchen to forage for a snack.

It hadn't been too much later when the telephone rang. Kevin answered it, and bellowed up the stairs for Kelly. She came clattering into the kitchen where

T. and her brother were looking at the newspaper, try-ing to decide which movie to take Kevin's girlfriend, Beth, and one of her friends to that night.

"It's your boyfriend," Kevin said in a purposely obnoxious high voice, and Kelly snatched the phone away, glaring dangerously at him.

She covered the mouthpiece. "Frank's not my boy-friend. He's a *friend* who happens to be a *boy,* and we're going to the prom together. So don't be a jerk."

On the phone, Frank sounded terrible. He had some kind of stomach virus, he told her. There was no way on earth he was going to make it to the prom.

Kelly slowly hung up the phone.

"What did Frankie want?" Kevin asked. "Can't decide between the sky-blue or the chartreuse tux?"

She wheeled, turning on him angrily. "When are you going to grow up? You're in graduate school, you're supposed to be an adult now, so why don't you act like one? Frank's sick, so I'm not going to the prom, all right? Does that satisfy your juvenile curi-osity? Or is there something else you want to know?"

"I'm sorry." Kevin was instantly contrite. "I didn't mean to be—"

"I'll take you," T. said.

"What?" Kevin and Kelly turned to him at the same time.

He was looking at Kelly, and he smiled his easy smile when their eyes met. "I mean, I'd *like* to take you."

Kevin stared at his friend in exasperation. "We're double-dating tonight. What, are you just going to blow off this friend of Beth's?"

"No." T. crossed his arms in front of him, and

leaned casually back in his chair. "I'll call her and tell her I can't make it."

"Because you want to take my little sister to some stupid high school dance?" Kevin laughed. "She's going to love that—"

"It's *not* a stupid dance," Kelly protested.

"Kev, it's her *prom*...."

Kevin sighed, looking from Kelly to Jax and back again. "Then I suppose *I* should take her."

"Gee, thanks," Kelly said. "A night out with Mr. Enthusiasm. I'd rather stay home."

But T. laughed, shaking his head. "No, Kev, you don't get it, do you? *I* want to take her. I *want* to take her. I would *love* to take her...."

Kelly swallowed. What was T. Jackson saying? She heard the words, but the implications were too intense.

T. turned and looked at her, his green eyes lit with an odd fire. "Kelly, will you let me take you to your prom?"

"Whoa, wait a minute," Kevin said before she could answer. He stared at his friend with growing realization, his voice tinged with disbelief. "Winchester, do you have, like, the *hots* for my little sister?"

But it was as if T. hadn't heard Kevin. He was just sitting there, his chair tipped back against the wall, smiling up at Kelly, waiting for her to answer him.

"Yeah." She'd smiled into his eyes as she'd nodded. "T., I'd really like that..."

Looking back now, Kelly knew that was the very moment she'd admitted to herself that she was in love with Tyrone Jackson Winchester the Second. And once she'd admitted it, she realized that she'd been in love with him for years. It wasn't puppy love. It wasn't a crush or an infatuation. It was solid, total, powerful love.

As she sat staring at her blank computer screen nearly seven years later, Kelly had to wonder.

What if T. had really been in love with her, too? What if they'd stayed together the way he'd promised, if he'd been the man she'd married when she was nineteen years old instead of Brad? Would her feelings have lasted?

Jax woke up drenched in sweat.

It was the nightmare again. The same old nightmare. He was back at that joke they'd called a trial.

He'd taken a flight from London a week earlier because the magazine he worked for had secured him a rare personal interview with the leader of the rebel forces in the tiny Central American country. The interview had gone smoothly and he had returned to his hotel room to type up his notes on his laptop computer.

Later that night he was roughly awakened by government soldiers and dragged to an official building where he was questioned about the location of the rebel forces. He'd been scared to death, but he refused to reveal even what little he knew about where he had been and who his contacts were.

Finally, after more than twenty-four hours of relentless questioning, he'd been released.

Back at the hotel, he'd considered calling the American consulate, telling them what had just happened, but there was a flight to Miami leaving almost immediately, and he barely had time to get to the airport, let alone make a phone call.

And he wanted to get out of there. Fast. He would have taken the next flight to Hades if he'd had to.

It was then, on his way to the plane, that the government's military police stopped his taxi. A quick search of his overnight bag led to the discovery of several large sacks of cocaine tucked neatly next to his underwear.

It was such an obvious frame-up that Jackson had laughed.

But as he sat in the ridiculous excuse for a courtroom the next day, listening to the announcement of the guilty verdict and the resulting ten-year jail sentence, he stopped laughing.

He'd managed to get in touch with the American consulate, but they could do nothing for him. Drug charges were out of their jurisdiction.

He was furious. It was so obvious. He was a reporter, he had information the government wanted. It was such a blatant setup. The drugs had been planted in his bag. What about his rights? He was an American—

But Jax had no rights, the consulate finally told him. He wasn't a hostage. He wasn't a political prisoner. He'd been convicted of possession of drugs, and there was nothing anyone could do to help him.

So he went to jail. He did not pass go, and he sure as hell didn't collect two hundred dollars.

Be good, the warden told him, and maybe you'll get out in five or six years.

It had been hell.

Jax had been put, alone, in a dark, damp cell with only a tiny slit of a window. He was let out only for an occasional meal or a walk around the compound. He might've gone crazy, and maybe he even did a little bit, because he started imagining Kelly. He started seeing her there with him, keeping him company, giving him strength. He had no paper, no pencil, but he still wrote hundreds of letters to Kelly. He wrote letters in his mind, letters that would never be sent, words he vowed he'd one day put onto paper.

And somehow he'd survived for twenty horrific months.

For years after, he'd had terrible nightmares, but finally they'd stopped.

So why was he dreaming about it again?

Chapter 3

After tipping the room-service waiter, Jax brought the breakfast tray to the table and set it down next to his computer. He poured himself a cup of steaming coffee and took a sip of the dark, pungent brew as he pulled his current story up on the computer screen.

Yesterday, when he'd finished writing, he'd left Jared in his horrible little room at the boardinghouse, fuming about the way Jax had spirited Carrie away from him.

Now. To get Jared on that boat for Europe.

Thinking hard, Jax took another sip of his coffee. He hadn't realized shipping Jared off to Europe was going to be this difficult. Jared was right—there was no way he would voluntarily leave Carrie, the way Jax had left Kelly all those years ago.

The two situations weren't exactly parallel, Jax reminded himself. Although Carrie and Kelly were both sixteen, back in Carrie's day, women frequently married at that age. And Jared wasn't Jax. Jared was a hero, while Jax was...only Jax.

He flipped through his notebook. In Jax's original outline, Jared had left Boston and gone to Europe, vowing to make his fortune and return a rich man, rich enough to wed the beautiful Carrie. But Jax had written that outline before he'd fleshed out the characters, before he knew just how bold and dauntless and damned self-confident Jared was going to be.

So now he was stuck with Carrie hidden away with some distant relatives, and Jared crossing his arms and refusing to leave until he found her.

How do you make a man do something he doesn't want to do?

Love.

No, it was because of love that Jared wanted to stick around.

Blackmail.

"Don't start with that dark family secret thing again," Jared said warningly.

"Cooperate, and I won't have to," muttered Jax.

That left money.

No, Jared had already said that he didn't need money to keep Carrie's heart.

What else?

Patriotism?

If Jared had the opportunity to make a fortune *and* at the same time help the Northern war effort...

England had provided weapons to the South during the Civil War. Despite the Northern blockades, English ships continued to smuggle guns to the Confederacy.

Enter Captain Reilly, the same old friend of Jared's father's who had appeared in chapters two and six, thought Jax with triumph. Reilly would offer Jared a chance to sail on his ship, to pirate the British vessels, seize their cargos and deliver the weaponry to the North—at a fair enough price to make a small fortune, of course.

Jax reached for his computer keyboard.

A sharp knock sounded on the door, rousing Jared from his sleep.

He sat up, his heart pounding as he stared into the darkness of his tiny room. Carrie, he thought. Carrie!

But even as he lit a candle, the knock sounded again, along with a familiar rusty voice. "Jared Dexter, you in there, boy? Open the damned door."

It was Captain Magnus Reilly, the owner of the ship called the *Graceful Lady Fair.*

Jax wrote quickly, bringing Captain Reilly into the room and letting the grizzled old man describe his plan to Jared.

"What do you say, Jared?" the captain asked. "Are you in? We've a chance to make a fortune."

Jared looked at Reilly in the flickering candlelight. Slowly he shook his head. "Sorry, old man," he said. "Not this time."

"No," Jax nearly shouted. "You're supposed to go with him, you fool. Don't you get it? It's your chance to serve your country *and* make some bucks. You'll come back rich, and then there's no way Carrie's family can refuse you.''

Jared crossed his arms obstinately. "I'm not going anywhere until I find Carrie.''

We'll see about that. Jax gritted his teeth as he deleted the last few sentences that he'd written.

Jared looked at Reilly in the flickering candle-light.

The boy's normally handsome, exuberant face looked pale and tired, thought the captain. And from the looks of things, he'd recently been in a fight.

"Magnus," Jared said slowly, "can you wait a few weeks? I can't leave the country right now.''

What was wrong with him today? Jax pressed the palms of his hands against the headache that was starting to throb behind his eyes.

In his mind, Jared smiled nastily at Jax. "*I* know what's wrong with you," he said, then uttered the words writers hate most to hear. "You've got writer's block.''

"I do not have writer's block," Jax said very calmly. "I simply have an obstinate, pigheaded, stubborn fool of a character who is refusing to cooperate.''

Jared sat back on his bed, lacing his fingers together behind his head. "Don't worry, the writer's block is only temporary,'' he returned with equal calm. "Work this thing out with Kelly and you'll be able to write again in no time, whether I cooperate or not.''

"Just tell Reilly you'll go with him." Jax ran his fingers tiredly through his hair. "Please?''

"Write me a love scene with Carrie and you've got a deal."

"Look, you're gonna have a happy ending," Jax promised. "I can guarantee that—"

"*That's* what's bothering you." Jared sat forward. "There's no guarantee that things are going to work out between you and Kelly. Bummer."

"Don't say 'bummer.' People in the nineteenth-century didn't say 'bummer.'" Jax took a deep breath. "Will you *please* go with Reilly?"

"My offer holds," Jared told him. "Write me that love scene and your wish is my command."

This was ridiculous. Jax readjusted the keyboard and began typing, refusing to be held hostage by his own character.

Without warning, Reilly pulled a revolver from under his jacket, pressing the cold metal of the barrel to Jared's head.

"You're coming with me, boy," he growled. "And you're coming now!"

Jared burst out laughing. "Wow, Jax," he said, between gasps for breath. "That's *really* stupid. There's absolutely *no* one who's going to believe that."

"Oh, shut up," Jax muttered. Cursing under his breath, he saved the job, turned off the laptop computer and went searching for some aspirin.

Dear Kelly,
You appear in my cell again today, and again, even though I know you can't possibly be real, I am thankful for your presence.

You are twelve years old this time, and as you

look around at the rough stone walls, at the damp
dirt floor and at the wooden bench and dirty straw
that I use for a bed, I can see anger in your dark
blue eyes.

You look me over just as carefully, taking in
my beard and my long, dirty hair.

You speak!

I can hear your husky voice clearly in the quiet
of the cell. Last time you visited, you didn't talk.
You only watched me.

"You smell," you tell me sternly, as if it were
my fault, and I apologize.

"Sometimes," I say, "when it rains, the
guards let us out with some scraps of soap and
we can wash—"

You are looking at me oddly, and I realize I
am speaking to you in Spanish. It's been so long
since I've heard an American voice. I translate,
and you nod.

"I guess it's been a while since it's rained,"
you say, sitting next to me on the straw.

"Soon it will do nothing but rain," I tell you,
"and there will be five inches of brackish water
on the floor of my cell."

You reach over and take my hand, holding it
tightly with your slender fingers.

I notice the scabs on your knees and elbows,
and you tell me about falling off of your bike.

I sympathize. I am careful to hide my own
healing wounds—three deep cuts from an irate
guard's whip that I earned by helping a fellow
prisoner to his feet when he stumbled on his way
to the courtyard for another endless roll-call
session.

But I can tell from looking into your eyes that you know. You also know about the broken rib I received from an earlier beating.

"I didn't cry," I tell you. "They can beat me, spit on me, treat me like less than an animal, but I will not cry. I hold my head up when I walk. I look them in the eye. I am the Americano, and they both hate me and respect me for that."

You look at me as if I am your hero, and for a few short hours, I am.

"Hey," you say, looking more closely at the walls, "igneous rocks."

We spend some time identifying and arguing about the rocks that were used in building this prison.

I almost forget where I am as I chip at the wall to get you a sample for your rock collection.

You leave when the sun hits the correct angle. For forty-seven minutes it will stream into my little window. A narrow strip of sunlight will travel across the wall, and I will stand in it, letting it shine on my dirty face. It gives me hope to know that only a few thousand miles away, that same powerful sun is shining on you.

I love you.

Love, T.

Jax leaned against the corridor wall outside the university classroom, waiting for Kelly.

This was probably a mistake. No, not probably. Definitely. Following Kelly around this way was definitely a mistake. She would definitely be annoyed. But Jax knew only one way to achieve success in life, and it involved a large amount of tenacity and a great deal of perseverance, and all the stubbornness he could muster, which could actually be quite a bit when it came down to it.

He was going to marry Kelly O'Brien. That much was certain.

What wasn't so clear was how he was going to deal with the fact that the bride-to-be didn't even want to have a cup of coffee with him.

After rejecting his offer of Chinese food five days ago, she'd turned him down the next day for lunch. He'd tried brunch the following day, and breakfast the day after that, with similar luck. Yesterday he was reduced to asking her out for coffee, for God's sake, and she'd turned that down, too.

So what was he doing here, waiting for her to come out of class? What was he going to invite her to do now? Go out with him for a glass of water?

Maybe it was time to start over again with dinner.

Sooner or later, she was going to give in.

She had told him once that she loved him. And if she had loved him even only a tenth as much as he loved her, he would bet his entire seven-figure bank account that those feelings hadn't totally disappeared.

The classroom door opened, and students spilled out into the hall. Good grief, they looked so young. Some of them were twelve years younger than he was. Had he really been their age once?

Kelly didn't see him as she came through the door.

She was wearing a denim workshirt with the sleeves rolled up, a worn-out pair of jeans and cowboy boots. Her hair was back in a single braid. Except for the hint of makeup on her face and lips, she looked almost exactly as she had when she was fourteen.

Except almost ten years older, thank God. Her jeans

hugged her body in a way that they never had when she was fourteen.

Jax followed her down the hall, not catching up with her until she stopped to swing open the big double doors that led into the building's main foyer.

Her eyes narrowed dangerously as she stared at him. "You're following me around," she said, not bothering to say hello.

"Yeah," he said, unperturbed.

She went into the foyer, moving out of the way of the steady stream of students who were going in and out of the doors. "Well, stop it," she said sternly. "You can tell Kevin that I'm really okay—"

"This has nothing to do with Kevin," Jax said, shaking his head. "I'm trying to get you to go out to dinner with me, Kel, and if you keep saying no, then you better get used to me following you around."

Kelly gazed at him. "Do you even *own* any socks?"

He looked down at his feet, lifting his pants slightly to get a better view of his bare ankles. "If I go back to my hotel and put on a pair of socks, will you have dinner with me?"

"I can't." She headed toward the doors that led out into the warm spring sunshine. "I have my last exam of the semester tomorrow."

"How about tomorrow night?" Jax followed her.

"How long are you going to be in town?" She stopped on the steps outside the building to fish in her backpack for her sunglasses.

As long as it takes. "At least a few more days." Jax put on his own sunglasses. "I've got some business to take care of on Friday, so…"

They began walking slowly down the sidewalk. The sun was hot on Jax's back, and he slipped off his jacket and rolled up his sleeves. "If you want, I could help you study tonight."

She slid him a sidelong glance. "For an advanced calculus exam?"

"Ouch." He winced. "Are you really taking calculus?"

"*Advanced* calculus."

"Yeah, right. Rub it in." He'd barely made it through trigonometry back in high school. And as an English major in college, he'd purposely stayed far, far away from the math building.

The sunlight glinted off his golden hair. With his dark sunglasses and his million-dollar smile, he looked like some kind of movie star. It was just Kelly's luck that T. Jackson had become better looking as he got older. Now, why couldn't he have thinning hair and a potbelly like some of Kevin's other old college friends?

"Why are you taking it?" he asked. "I mean, I've never known you to be a masochist."

She shot him a quick look, but he didn't realize the irony of his words. He was right, she wasn't a masochist, and that was one of the reasons she didn't want him hanging around.

"I'm taking it because I like science, and calculus is a prerequisite for some of the advanced science courses I want to take next year," she told him. Her cowboy boots made a clicking sound against the concrete sidewalk. "I'm sorry, T.," she added, "but I don't think you'll be any help as a study partner."

"It's been years since you've seen me," he protested. "How do you know I haven't suddenly become a math whiz?"

Kelly burst out laughing.

"How many more semesters do you have before you graduate?" he asked.

"Three," Kelly said. "I married Brad when I was a sophomore. Appropriate, huh?"

Marrying Brad had been incredibly sophomoric. She'd thought she knew what she was doing, what she wanted, but in reality, she had had absolutely no idea, not one clue. And apparently Brad hadn't known what he'd really wanted, either.

"We moved to California that summer," she told T. Jackson, "and there wasn't enough time for me to transfer to a school out there. So I got a job, and by the time the spring semester started, Brad had been laid off and we really needed the money."

"Are you going to take this summer off," he asked, "or do you have a job lined up?"

She shrugged. "Nothing definite. I've interviewed at a couple of places."

"Spend the summer on the Cape with me."

Kelly stopped walking. "What?"

"I live out on Cape Cod," T. Jackson said. He took off his sunglasses. She could see from his eyes that he was actually serious. "I've got a house on the beach, on the bay side, in Dennis. It's this huge modern monster—we've got lots of extra bedrooms, there's plenty of room." He stopped, laughed softly, shaking his head. "Look, I'd love to spend some time with you, and…"

"I won't even go out to dinner with you," Kelly told him. "What on earth makes you think I'd want to spend the entire summer with you on the Cape?"

He put his sunglasses back on. "I don't know," he said. "You always wanted to. You talked about it all the time, and I just thought…"

"I was *twelve*, T." She wasn't being completely truthful. She'd talked about it when she was older than twelve, too. Dreamed about it. A summer at the Winchester compound on the Cape.

Kelly stared up at him, seeing her face reflected in the lenses of his sunglasses. Truth was, spending the summer on the beach with T. Jackson would fulfill just about every single one of her childhood fantasies. And quite a few of her teenaged fantasies, too.

But as an adult, she knew her fantasies about T. were simply that. Fantasies. She knew what kind of man he was, because she'd been married to a man exactly like him. She no longer had any illusions about living happily ever after with T. Jackson, no matter how charming and handsome and sexy he was.

If she wanted happily ever after—and she did—she was going to have to find a different type of man. She'd gladly trade some of the spark, the sexual chemistry, for a man who would love only her. She wanted a man who gave as much as he took, a man who truly knew how to love, not just *be* loved. A man who kept his promises.

But there was something to be said for spending a few months with T. Jackson Winchester the Second. It would be one *hell* of a summer, that was for sure.

Unless this was just another of his favors to Kevin...

She could just imagine the conversation her brother must've had with T. "Cheer her up," Kevin must've told Jax. "Take her out, show her a good time. She used to have a crush on you, remember? Make her feel important. If anyone can do it, you can."

But it hadn't been a crush. What she had felt for T. Jackson had been so much more than a crush. And did she really want to wreck her romantic memories of her first love by going and having a tawdry affair with the man?

When the answer didn't come as an immediate no, Kelly shook her head in disgust. What was wrong with her?

"I'm going to be busy all summer," she said, starting down the sidewalk again. And she would be. When she finished writing her second novel, she'd start on a third. It was a never-ending process, but one that she loved. And right now her writing was a way to stay safe, insulated from the rest of the world. And from T. Jackson Winchester the Second in particular.

"Think about it," he said.

The annoying thing was, she would. In fact, she'd probably think about nothing else. She'd probably dream about spending the entire summer with T. He'd already appeared in her dreams last night, her imagination clothing him in a hell of a lot less than the bathing suit he'd wear as a standard uniform on the Cape. Her subconscious was giving her a very deliberate message—there was unfinished business between the two of them.

But it was a hormonal thing. It was pure sex, and it had nothing to do with love. Even if she ended up giving in to T.'s persistent demands, even if she ended up sleeping with the man, she'd never let him back into her heart. Never.

"So are we on for dinner tomorrow night?" Jax asked as they stopped outside the school newspaper office door.

"Tomorrow night?" She shook her head. "I don't—"

"Friday night, then."

"No," she said definitely. "I'm going to a meeting in the late afternoon. I don't know how long it'll last."

"I've got something happening Friday afternoon, too," he said. "We can eat later—"

"No."

Jax looked at her, silent for a moment. Then he laughed. "I guess I'm going to have to keep following you around, then."

Kelly took off her sunglasses, sighing with exasperation. "Jackson—"

He kissed her.

It was little more than a light brushing of his lips against hers, but it was a kiss. And it was enough to make her system go haywire. She stared at him in shock.

"See you tomorrow, Kel." He smiled and walked away.

Jared was right. Jax realized it would be much more romantically tragic if Carrie were whisked away to the safety of distant relatives *after* she and Jared had a scene in which they planned to run away together. Jax just wasn't convinced it should be a love scene.

"She's only sixteen," he muttered. "She's too young."

"That's a load of crap, and you know it," Jared countered. "Just because *you* made the mistake of thinking that *Kelly* was too young—"

"She *was* too young."

"You ran because you knew you couldn't deny her anything," Jared said. "You knew if you stayed, you'd make love to her, because she wanted you to. You left because you were scared."

"I left because I loved her!" Jax argued.

"You didn't even have the decency to tell her you were going—"

"Because what Kevin threatened to do was—"

"So what are you saying?" Jared's dark eyes were intense. "Are you saying that you want *me* to make the same stupid mistake you did? I thought one of the reasons you were writing this story was to give yourself a chance to do it over, and do it *right* this time."

"Fine!" Jax threw up his hands. "I'll write that love scene. But I've got to warn you, friend. It's only going to be one night. And things are going to get much worse before you get your happy ending. I've got another 230 pages to fill."

Jax sat in his sports car. From where he was parked, he could see light streaming from the front window of Kelly's apartment.

He'd left his hotel room this evening after writing a passionate scene between Jared and Carrie. Writing sensual scenes made him restless, in need of air. He'd intended to go to a movie, but somehow he'd wound up here.

He'd waited for Kelly this afternoon as she finished up her calculus exam. He'd asked her to go out to dinner again, and again she refused. This time he could barely keep up with her as she nearly ran to the newspaper office. She'd disappeared inside with only a quick goodbye, not giving him enough time to kiss her again.

God, he wanted to kiss her. He wanted to kiss her the way Jared had kissed Carrie in the scene he'd written only a few hours ago. Jax wanted to kiss Kelly the way he had on that night so many years ago—prom night....

At first Kevin had refused to let Jax take Kelly to the school dance. He'd followed Jax all the way downtown, to the tux rental place. A little bell had tinkled as they walked into the air-conditioned interior of the tiny shop.

"I need a tux," Jax told the skinny man behind the counter.

"No, he doesn't," Kevin countered, folding his big arms across his beefy chest. "*I* need a tux." He turned to Jax. "She's too young for you."

The shopkeeper removed a measuring tape from around his neck, and stood looking at them. "You both want tuxes?"

"No." Jax smiled. "Just me."

"No." The fierceness of Kevin's voice was a sharp contrast to Jax's cool control. "Not him. Me. I need it for tonight."

"I'm taking her," Jax said mildly to Kevin. He leaned against a glass-topped counter that held an assortment of bow ties and cummerbunds.

"She's a *kid*." Kevin's face was pink with anger. "You should be dating women, not little girls."

"Don't you trust me?" Jax asked, his voice level.

"No, not after the way I saw you looking at her this afternoon." Kevin ran his hands through his short red hair in exasperation as he glared up at his friend. "Hell, Winchester, she's only sixteen!"

"I know how old she is."

"You better keep that in mind. She's jailbait, pal." Kevin took a threatening step forward, stabbing Jax's chest with his forefinger. But Jax didn't move a muscle, didn't even blink. "You mess with her," Kevin threatened, "and you'll end up in prison. And I'll personally escort you there."

The two young men locked gazes for several long moments. Then Jax smiled, shaking his head slightly. "You know I'd never do anything to hurt her, Kev."

"Mess with Kelly and I'll kill you," Kevin repeated, but the anger was gone from his voice.

"I'm crazy about her," Jax admitted. "I'll take good care of her, I promise."

"You *are* crazy." Kevin laughed with disbelief. "Beth has a gorgeous friend who's dying to get naked with you, but *you* want to go out with a girl who's barely out of diapers. I just don't get it."

Jax smiled. "You don't have to get it. Just relax. I want to go out with Kelly tonight, and you want to go out with Beth. We're both doing each other a favor, okay?"

"I still think you're nuts."

Jax looked at the shopkeeper, who was watching them with unabashed interest. "I need a tux for tonight," he said again.

But the shopkeeper shook his head. "What're you? Six foot five? I'm sorry, no can do. I only had a few rental tuxes in your size, and they're out. Won't be back in 'til Sunday."

"Then I'll buy one," Jax said.

"You'll what?" Kevin's eyebrows disappeared under his thick red hair.

Jax smiled at his friend. "I'll buy one." He looked back at the shopkeeper. "And I'll pay extra if you get the alterations done by this afternoon."

By five o'clock, Jax had showered, shaved and finished putting on his brand-new tuxedo up in Kevin's room. He didn't remember being this excited about going to his own junior prom.

Kelly's door was still closed, so he headed downstairs to wait for her. Jax stopped in the kitchen first, pulling the flowers he'd bought her out of the refrigerator and carrying them into the living room.

Nolan O'Brien was lying on the couch, reading the newspaper as Jax came in, and he looked over the top of it, smiling. Kevin and Kelly's father was an older, heavier version of Kevin. He had the same red-orange hair, thinning a bit on top, though, the same beefy frame, the same cheerful disposition and millions and millions of the same freckles.

"So you're the sacrificial substitute date for the prom, eh?" the older man asked, not bothering to move from his relaxed position on the couch.

"It's no sacrifice, Nolan," Jax said easily, sitting down in the rocking chair that was across from the couch. He leaned forward to put the flowers on the coffee table.

"A corsage *and* a dozen roses," Nolan said, looking at Jax appraisingly with a slow smile. "I was wondering when you were going to start noticing that Kelly's almost all grown up. Looks like it finally happened."

Jax smiled.

Nolan folded the newspaper. "I suppose I don't have to give you the normal 'date speech' that I give the rest of the boys that take Kelly out—you know, the 'no drinking and driving' speech, the 'get her home before midnight' speech…"

"I know your rules," Jax said, nodding. "Although you might want to cut loose with the curfew for tonight. Kelly told me there are after-prom parties scheduled one after the other until sun-up. And then, if it's warm enough, everyone's heading over to the beach."

Nolan nodded. "Okay," he said agreeably, swinging himself up into a sitting position. "Just don't forget, Kelly comes across as being much older than she really is. Keep in mind that she's only sixteen. There's a big difference between sixteen and twenty-two, Jax."

The older man's eyes were intense. Jax smiled, realizing that Nolan was giving him a polite version of the same message Kevin had delivered at the tuxedo shop: Don't mess with Kelly.

"I know," Jax said quietly.

"Good."

Ten minutes later, Kelly was sitting next to Jax in his little red Spitfire, and they were heading down the road toward town, toward the restaurant where he had made dinner reservations.

Jax glanced over at her, still struck by how beautiful, how elegant and poised she looked.

When she'd appeared in the living room, his heart had nearly stopped.

She was wearing that fabulous blue gown, and her hair was pinned up, swept back loosely, femininely, from her face. She was wearing makeup and her eyes looked more blue than they ever had before, with her long, dark lashes accentuated. Her normally pretty, fresh face looked exotically beautiful with her hair up, giving Jax a good look at the gorgeous woman she was destined to become in the next few years.

Kelly was a child-woman, a curious mixture of innocence and poise, elegance and enthusiasm. She was unconsciously sexy—well, maybe not entirely unconsciously. She wasn't wearing a bra beneath her slinky gown because the back of the dress was open. True, the top wasn't tight fitting, but the smooth material occasionally clung to her lithe body, and the effect was…extremely distracting.

He'd thought he'd have no trouble taking her out like this. He'd thought after four years of being close friends with Kelly that it wouldn't be hard to remember she was still only a kid.

So why was it that he could think of little else but how her lips would feel against his?

Jackson's pulse was running too fast, his heart pounding. Relax, he ordered himself, forcing himself to breathe slowly. Just relax. Stay cool.

"This feels…strange," Kelly said, glancing at T. from beneath her eyelashes. She laughed softly. "You look as tense as I feel."

"I'm not tense," Jax protested, reaching up with one hand to loosen the tight muscles in the back of his neck. "Are you tense?"

"Yeah," she admitted with her usual candor and a brief, charming smile. "I just keep thinking…well… maybe we should go Dutch tonight."

"Dutch?" he said, disbelief in his voice as he looked over at her. "Nope. This is on me, Kel."

"It doesn't seem fair to make you pay for everything—" she turned slightly in the bucket seat to face him "—just because I happen to be female. Especially considering that I shanghaied you."

"Do I look like I'm suffering?" Jax asked, amused.

"You never look like you're suffering. That's why it's so hard to tell whether or not you actually *are*."

"I'll let you know if and when I start," he assured her with a grin as he pulled up to a red light.

She looked up at him, and he returned her gaze. Her face was so familiar. He knew her so well. Or did he? He knew the child, not the woman. And sometime during the past few months, she'd suddenly become part woman. Her skin looked so smooth, so pale compared to the inky darkness of her hair. Yet her cheeks were flushed with a soft glow of good health, her mouth curved up into a small smile, her eyes bright, sparking as they met his own. Jax could imagine himself drowning in the blue depths of her eyes. Imagine? Hell, he *was* drowning.

A short beep from the car behind him told him that the light had changed, and he forced his eyes back to the road. After a moment, he glanced quickly at Kelly, but she was looking down at the small clutch purse she was holding in her lap, a faint tinge of embarrassment on her cheeks.

God, she knew everything he was feeling just from looking into his eyes. He'd learned a long time ago that he couldn't hide things from Kelly, so why should he expect to be able to hide this?

The main problem, was that he wasn't exactly sure what ''this'' was.

Was he in love with her?

If he wasn't in love with her already, he was definitely teetering. No, not just teetering, he'd already lost his balance. There was nowhere for him to go but over the edge.

Kelly glanced at him again, smiling, and Jax felt a sudden lack of gravity deep in the pit of his stomach.

Free fall. He was in free fall, there was no doubt about it. He'd taken the plunge, and he was falling hard and fast.

Add into the equation all the feelings he was already carrying around for Kelly. It was one hell of an emotional attachment, and one he couldn't deny. Add to *that* this explosively intense physical attraction…

If she were eighteen years old, he would court her ruthlessly. He would use every trick in the book to get her to fall in love with him, too. He would take her out, buy her presents—hell, he'd even seduce her. He would tell her and show her in every way possible that he loved her. He would make love to her endlessly. And then he would get down on his knees and beg her to marry him.

God, he actually wanted to *marry* her, as in 'til death do us part, as in happily ever after. There was just one problem. She wasn't eighteen years old. She was sixteen. Jailbait, as Kevin had so indelicately put it.

For one wild moment Jax wondered if Nolan and Lori O'Brien would give their daughter permission to marry him now. But as quickly as the thought entered his mind, he pushed it away. It wouldn't happen. Kelly's parents would never agree to it. They would say that she wasn't old enough. And they would be right.

There was just no getting around it. Kelly was too young.

That left him only one option. He'd simply have to wait for her to get older.

"This *is* strange," Kelly said. "I think this is the first time I've ever seen you so quiet." She laughed softly. "Usually I can't shut you up."

"Sorry," Jax said. "I was thinking."

"About the job offer you got from that London magazine?"

He looked over to find her watching him, her face serious. "What do you think about that? Should I take it?"

She was quiet for so long, he thought maybe she

wasn't going to answer. But when he glanced back at her, she was still watching him steadily.

"I can't answer that fairly," she finally said. "See, when I think about it, I can find all kinds of reasons why you *should* take that job. I mean, come on, T., you'd be living in *London*. That would be so great. You could spend your vacations in Europe." She looked away from him, out the window, at the spring wildflowers that were growing along the sides of the road. "It's true it's not a lot of money," she continued, "but you'd be paid to write. After a couple of years as a staff writer for the magazine, you'd have name recognition, so if you ever started working on that novel you keep talking about, you'd probably have an easier time selling it."

She was quiet, and he glanced at her again. "But..." he prompted her.

"I'd miss you," Kelly said simply. "That's why I can't answer your question fairly. I don't want you to live on the other side of the Atlantic Ocean."

Happiness exploded inside of Jackson. "Then I won't go. I'll find a job in Boston."

"Tyrone, don't tease."

"I'm serious."

"But—" she started, then stopped, her eyes widening as Jackson pulled his sports car into the parking lot of the Breckenridge Inn, the fanciest restaurant in the area. "Whoa, T., what's this?"

"This is where we're having dinner." Jax pulled into a parking space at the edge of the big lot.

"But this is too expensive—"

"You're worth every penny."

"I would've settled for Bertucci's," she said.

"Why settle?" Jax pulled up the parking brake and turned off the engine as he smiled at her.

Kelly's eyes danced with delight. "Why don't you have women falling all over you, T.?" she asked. "You're so smooth, you put James Bond to shame."

"It's the name." Jax sighed. "Winchester," he said in his best Sean Connery. "Tyrone Jackson Winchester the Second… No, see, my name's way too long. By the time I finish saying my name, all the gorgeous women have either fallen asleep or they've gone off with the guy with the shorter name."

Kelly laughed again and Jax glanced at the dashboard. The digital clock read 5:35. The prom didn't start until eight o'clock. There were two hours and twenty-five minutes before he could dance with Kelly, before he could hold her in his arms. He wasn't sure he would survive until then.

Of course, compared to the four hundred and fifty-nine days he had to wait until she turned eighteen, two hours and twenty-five minutes was a piece of cake.

She was looking at him, her lips moist and parted slightly. God, he wanted to kiss her. God, he wanted to…

"Shall we go inside?" he asked, opening his door. But Kelly put her hand on his arm. Even through his jacket and shirt, her soft touch made him freeze.

"Jackson—" she began to say, then stopped, pulling her hand back onto her lap.

"Uh-oh." Jax tried to be light, turning toward her. "You only call me that when you mean business. What'd I do?"

Kelly shook her head. "There's something I want to ask you, and I'm not really sure how to."

"You've never had a problem being direct before. Just ask."

She looked down at her hands for a moment, then shook her head again, laughing softly. "This is stupid, but…" She looked up at him. "Is this a real date?"

Kelly was looking directly into his eyes, and again Jax had the sensation of drowning. He was being pulled under again. Sooner or later, he was going to go down, and he wouldn't make it back up. "I think so," he said slowly. "What's the definition of a real date?"

She moistened her lips with the tip of her tongue, and Jackson's eyes were drawn to her mouth. He couldn't look away—he was hypnotized.

"A real date is when you go out with someone that you like enough to kiss good-night when it's over," Kelly said softly.

When, oh when, did the inside of his car get so tiny?

Jax pulled his eyes away from the delicately shaped lips that were only a few scant inches from his own mouth. "Yeah," he managed to say. "This is a real date."

"Could you—" Kelly said haltingly. "Could we—" She laughed self-consciously and started again. "T., this is going to sound really weird, but the thought of kissing you is making me really nervous and—"

"Then I won't kiss you," he said quickly.

"No, that's not what—" She shook her head, laughing again. "See, I was just thinking if you kissed me *now,* I could stop being nervous about it."

"Now," Jackson repeated. He held on tightly to the steering wheel, afraid that if he let go, he'd lose his balance. She wanted him to kiss her. Now.

''I mean, it would take some of the pressure off, don't you think?''

No. No, he did not think that it would take any kind of pressure off at all. Not for him, anyway. Still, when he looked into her eyes, he knew there was no way on earth he could turn her down.

He felt himself lean toward her, closer, closer. He reached out his hand to cup her face. Her skin was so soft underneath his fingers. He ran his thumb across her lips.

Jax could feel his heart pounding in his chest. He was going to be the first twenty-two-year-old to die of a love-induced heart attack. He smiled. There were certainly worse ways to go.

Kelly returned his smile, then closed her eyes, lifting her lips to him. He moved that final fraction of an inch, and then he was kissing her.

Her mouth felt warm and soft as he slowly, gently brushed his own lips across hers. It took every ounce of control he had to keep himself from deepening the kiss, to keep himself from touching her lips with his tongue, from entering her sweet mouth.

Breathing hard, he pulled back to look at her. Her breasts were rising and falling as if she, too, were having trouble pulling air into her lungs.

''T., don't stop,'' she whispered, and he groaned, knowing he shouldn't kiss her again, knowing he *should* stop right here and right now before this got out of hand.

''Please,'' she whispered, and everything he knew he should do went right out the window as he bent his head to kiss her again.

This time her arms went up around his neck. He felt her fingers in his hair as their lips met. He felt her mouth open underneath his, her tongue lightly touch his lips.·

He swept his arms around her, pulling her against his chest as he gently met her tongue with his own. He wanted to pull her over the parking brake onto his lap, to reach under her light spring shawl to cup her breasts in the palms of his hands. He wanted to kiss her long and hard and deep, and he wanted to keep kissing her until she turned eighteen. And then he wanted to make love to her. He wanted to be her first lover, and her last.

"Kelly," he said between kisses, his voice raspy and thick. "Kelly—"

He had to do it. He had to kiss her just once the way he was dying to. Just one real kiss.

He swept his tongue into her mouth, fiercely, wildly, claiming her, possessing her. He could feel her fingers tighten in his hair as she pulled him even closer to her, as she met his kiss with a passion that equaled his own.

One kiss became two, then three, then more, and suddenly nothing else mattered or even existed. There was only Kelly. Kelly, who knew him better than anyone in the world. Kelly, with whom he shared all of his secrets. All of his secrets, including this one—he loved her, the way a man loves a woman.

But faintly he was aware that time was passing, and somehow, somewhere, he found strength to pull away from her sweet lips.

"Oh, T.," she breathed, "I've never been kissed like that before."

He closed his eyes, still holding her in his arms, her head against his shoulder as waves of emotion flooded him. It was an odd combination of relief and guilt and love, happiness and great sorrow, all mixed together, blended in a confusing blur.

He held her for what seemed like hours, until his pulse slowed. When it reached as close as he thought it would get to normal for that evening, he released her.

His hands shook as he tried to get the keys out of the ignition, and he dropped them on the floor. He took a deep breath and combed his hair back with his fingers, then turned to look at Kelly.

She smiled as he met her eyes. "Well, I guess you're not gay."

Jax stared at her, momentarily floored. "What did you just say?" he asked in a burst of air, even though he knew he'd heard her correctly.

"A few days ago, Christa asked me if you were gay."

"You're kidding." Christa was Kelly's aunt who had lived with the O'Briens that same summer that Jax had.

"She's been wondering for a while why you don't have a girlfriend. I told her I didn't know what your sexual preference was," Kelly said with a nonchalant shrug.

"*Kel*ly!" Jax's voice reached up an octave in outrage before he saw the amusement sparkling in her eyes, before the smile she was trying to hide crept out.

"Relax, Jackson. I told her that you were straight...but I don't think she believed me. She's very big on proof, and frankly, I didn't have any."

This conversation was getting *way* out of hand. And the clock on the dashboard now read 6:03. Man, had he really sat here in his car for the past half hour making out with Kevin's little sister? Someone was surely saving a place for him in hell, because that was right where he was going to go after Kevin broke his neck.

And Kelly was looking at him as though she didn't want to get out of the car for at least another half an hour.

"Kelly, let's have dinner," he said desperately, his usual cool demeanor slipping. "Please?"

With a smile, she adjusted the rearview mirror and carefully reapplied her lipstick. Jax couldn't bear to watch, afraid he wouldn't be able to keep himself from kissing it off her lips, too.

He forced himself out of the car, picked his keys up off the floor, then went around to open Kelly's door. He offered her his hand to help her out, and she put her slim, cool fingers into his as she smiled up at him. He caught a quick, breathtaking glimpse of her shapely legs through the slit in her skirt and then she was out of the car. He closed the door behind her, reminding himself to keep breathing.

As they crossed the gravel driveway to the front entrance, Kelly slipped her hand into the crook of Jax's arm. He covered her hand with his, unable to keep himself from lightly stroking the tops of her fingers.

"T.," she said quietly as they approached the door to the restaurant. He looked down into her steady blue gaze. "It didn't really help, did it?"

She was talking about those practice good-night kisses. With a laugh, Jax shook his head. "No, Kel, it sure didn't."

"Well, at least I'm not nervous anymore," she said with a small smile.

Yeah, but Jax still was. In fact, now he was *twice* as nervous.

Chapter 4

Dear Kelly,

Another day dawns and I am still here in this damned miserable cell.

One of the guards takes pity on me and slips me some American paperback books that were left behind in the hotel where his wife works as a maid.

There are three of them—all romances. One is a long historical, the other two are shorter and set in the present day. I read them eagerly, voraciously, in the dim light from my little window. I read them over and over again, taking great joy in the happy endings, the tender embraces of the lovers reunited at last.

You come after sunset, when it's too dark to read any longer, and I proudly show the books to you. They are my prize possessions, and I keep them carefully out of sight of the other guards.

Tonight you are sixteen, and you leaf through the books casually in the darkness, far more interested in the paper they are printed on than the words themselves.

"If you write really small," you tell me, "you can use this paper and write between the lines."

I stare at you stupidly.

You laugh. "T., you always said that you'd write a novel if you could only find the time," you say. You lift one eyebrow humorously. "Well, suddenly you've got plenty of time."

I am elated, but only briefly. "I have nothing to write with."

"Ask the guard who gave you these books. Ask him for a pencil or a pen."

"I will."

You smile, and I suddenly realize you are wearing your prom dress. You are so beautiful, my heart nearly stops beating.

You lean forward to kiss me, and I can feel your soft lips, smell your perfume. You take me with you, back in time, and for a while, I am out of my cell. I sit with you in my sports car, clean-shaven and smelling sweet, wearing my tuxedo, and we kiss.

You are still so young, and I'm even older now, and I still don't know better. I still can't stop myself.

I love you.

Love, T.

It was well past 2:00 a.m. by the time Kelly shut down her computer and turned off the lights in her apartment. She moved to the living room window, remembering that she hadn't closed and locked it the way she did every night. As she pulled the window down, the sound of a car's engine starting out on the street caught her attention. As she watched, a sleek sports car pulled away from the curb, dimly lit by the streetlight on the corner. She looked closer, sure that she could see the glint of golden hair through the driver's side window.

The first thing she felt was anger. What the *hell* was T. doing, spying on her until all hours of the night?

But it didn't take long for rational thought to intercede. He couldn't have been spying on her. The only way he could have seen into her windows was if he'd somehow gained access to the apartment across the street. And it was hardly likely that he had gone to such lengths. If he had wanted to know what she was doing, he would've no doubt simply knocked on her door.

So then, what *was* he doing? Sitting out in his car in front of her house for God only knows how many hours?

Why?

The only answer she could come up with was more than a bit alarming. It had to be the physical attraction, the same old irresistible pull that they had nearly given in to on her prom night, so many years ago. *She* still felt it tugging at her every time he was near. No doubt he did, too.

Kelly lay back in her bed and threw her arm across her eyes. She was exhausted, but sleep didn't come. Finally, too tired to fight, she closed her eyes and let her memories carry her back in time to that wonderful, terrible Saturday night of the prom.

She couldn't begin to remember what she ate for dinner at the Breckenridge Inn. She wasn't sure that she even knew at the time. Her attention had been so totally captured by T. Jackson Winchester the Second....

He'd reached across the table between courses, holding her hand lightly, playing with her fingers, making her think about the way he had kissed her in the car. He'd kept up a steady stream of conversation about books, movies, music, anything and everything, but there had been an odd fire in his eyes that had let her know he, too, had been thinking about kissing her again.

When the waiter brought their dinners, he also brought them each a complimentary glass of white wine. T. looked at Kelly, one eyebrow slightly raised, but he said nothing until the waiter left.

"People always think I'm older than I am," she said. "It was a drag back when I was eleven. I used to get into arguments with the ticket lady at the movie theater. I finally had to bring her my birth certificate to prove that I really was under thirteen." She smiled. "But now I'd say it's paying off." She toyed with the long stem of her wineglass. "I wish, at least, that I was eighteen."

T. was leaning back lazily in his chair, his handsome face lit by flickering candlelight. "I wish you were, too."

"I feel like I'm spending all of my time waiting." Kelly gazed into the stormy gray-green of his eyes. "I know exactly what I want to do, I know exactly what I want from life, but it's going to be another few years before I'm allowed to start living."

"Four hundred and fifty-nine days."

She looked at him in surprise.

He smiled. "I'm counting." He leaned forward suddenly. "What *do* you want from life?" His eyes were electric green now, and they seemed to shine in the dim light, intense, piercing.

You.

She almost said it aloud. Instead she said, "I want what I've always wanted, the same thing you want—to be a writer."

"So do it," T. told her. "Be a writer. Just because you're living at home, just because you're still in high school, doesn't mean you can't start sending your stories out to magazines. It doesn't mean you can't get published. If you really want something, if you've really figured out what you want, then go for it, work for it, do it. Don't hold back. No matter what else you do, just keep writing."

His face was so serious. A lock of hair had fallen across his forehead, but he didn't bother to push it back. Kelly gazed at his perfect features—perfect except for the tiny scar below his left eye, close to his temple, on his cheekbone. He'd been in a fight in high school, he'd once told her, being purposely vague.

That scar had always been a reminder to Kelly that there was more to T. Jackson than he'd let the world believe from his cool and collected outward appearance. There was a fire inside of him, ready to spark into flames if he was pressed hard enough.

She'd tasted that fire when he'd kissed her. But even when he kissed her so passionately, she'd felt his control, felt him holding back. She'd never seen him when he wasn't in control, and had only rarely seen him rattled. She smiled again, remembering his reaction when she'd mentioned that Christa doubted his masculinity. But still, even then, he'd really only been slightly fazed.

That scar, though, was proof that there was a side to T. that she'd hadn't yet seen. And although the scar interrupted the lines of his face, it added a mysteriousness and an unpredictability to him, and Kelly found that wonderfully, dangerously attractive.

As he gazed across the table at her, his eyes held the same fiery fierceness that Kelly had seen right before he had kissed her in the car—those amazing, industrial-strength kisses. As she watched, he forced his eyes away from her, down to his plate, and stared at the food in front of him as if he hadn't realized it was there.

If you really want something, he had said, *if you've really figured out what you want…*

She wanted T., there was no doubt about it. And she wanted him forever. It couldn't be much clearer to her, it couldn't be more obvious.

Then go for it…don't hold back.

"There's more," she said quietly, and he looked up at her. There was uncertainty in his eyes, and she realized he wasn't following. "There's more that I want," she explained.

As she watched, understanding replaced the confusion. As she gazed at him, she saw his sudden comprehension, along with a renewed flare of the fire that was burning inside of him.

I want you.

She didn't have to say the words. He knew.

He smiled at her, but it was tinged with sadness. "Oh, Kel," he whispered. "What am I going to do about this?"

She picked up her fork and toyed with the food on

her plate for a moment before she answered. "You could start by asking me out on another date."

He reached across the table, lacing her fingers with his. "What are you doing tomorrow night?"

Kelly felt her heart flip-flop. He was taking her seriously. "I've got nothing planned."

"Will you go to a movie with me?" he asked. "We could get something to eat before or after, depending on what time the movie starts."

Kelly looked down at her barely touched dinner and laughed. "Maybe we should skip the meal. Neither of us seems to care much about food these days."

"Is that a yes?" His hand tightened slightly on hers.

"Yes."

"Will you go out with me Monday night, too?"

"Yes."

"Tuesday?"

Kelly laughed. "Yes."

"How about Wednesday?"

"I'm supposed to baby-sit for the Wilkinses. You know, they live down the street."

"I remember," Jax said. "Kevin and I filled in over there for you last year when you got that virus. Do you think they would mind if I came along?"

"No," Kelly told him.

"Good." Jax smiled. "Then that just leaves Thursday and Friday...and every other night for the next one year and ninety-four days. Will you go out with me those nights, too?"

As Kelly gazed into his warm green eyes, she was incredibly, deliriously happy. "Yes," she whispered.

He brought her hand up to his lips, gently kissing the tips of her fingers. "Good."

"Why only a year and ninety-four days?" she wondered aloud.

He lifted her hand to his mouth again, this time kissing her palm. Kelly inhaled sharply at the sensation, and heat raced through her body. She could see the same heat in T.'s eyes as the warm green turned hot. "Because in one year and ninety-four days, you'll be eighteen."

"What happens then?" She watched, mesmerized as he kissed the soft inside of her wrist, pressing her throbbing pulse with his lips.

"Lots of things," he replied, watching her through half-closed eyelids. His thumb now traced slow circles on the palm of her hand, and Kelly felt nearly overpowered by her feelings. She wanted to kiss him again. She wanted...

She knew about sex, even though she had no experience. She'd read plenty of books, seen movies, heard talk, but she'd never really quite understood what the big deal was all about. Until now.

"When you're eighteen, you'll start college," Jackson was saying lazily, still smiling at her. "You'll leave home. You'll marry me."

Kelly pulled her hand free. "Tyrone, don't tease about something like that."

"I'm not teasing."

She looked up at him. His smile was gone. Kelly felt a rush of dizziness, and she started to laugh. "I thought, according to convention, that a man is supposed to *ask* a woman to marry him, not simply *tell* her that she will."

"Oh, I'll ask," Jax had said. "The minute you turn eighteen, Kelly, I'm going to ask...."

But he hadn't. Even though he had disappeared a

few days after the prom, even though he had broken all of the other promises he had made to her that night, Kelly had spent her entire eighteenth birthday waiting for him to show up, to call, to come for her.

But he never had.

Tears still stung her eyes as she remembered the bitter disappointment, the hurt. It was on that day she convinced herself that she had truly stopped loving T. Jackson Winchester the Second. It was on that day that she started moving ahead with her life. It was the day she finally agreed to go out with Brad Foster.

It was better it had happened this way. Better that she'd married Brad instead of T. Because although finding Brad with another woman had hurt her, it wasn't the end of the world. It was simply the end of their relationship.

But if it had been T. Jackson she had found in bed with someone else…that would have destroyed her. Her heart would never have recovered.

Now that Jared was cooperating, Jax's writing should have been going much more smoothly. But it wasn't.

Oh, he managed to write, but it was like pulling teeth, rather than the effortless, almost stream-of-consciousness outpouring of words he was used to.

He sent Jared off to sea for close to two long, dangerous years. But as his hero was triumphantly returning to Boston a wealthy man, the *Graceful Lady Fair* was taken for a British ship and attacked by the Union fleet. Instead of reclaiming Carrie, Jared was wounded and mistakenly sent to a prison camp for Confederate soldiers. It took him another year and a half, and about

100 pages, to recover from his injuries and successfully escape the prison.

But then, finally, *finally* Jared was in Boston.

With a spring in his step, Jared walked down the
street that led to the Sinclairs' town house. He
hadn't felt this good, this *whole,* in years. It
wouldn't be long now before he held Carrie in
his arms....

Jax stopped typing, his fingers poised on the keyboard.

Jared tapped his foot impatiently. "What's the matter? What are you waiting for?"

"You're not going to like this," Jax muttered.

Jared froze. "Don't tell me she's not here."

"She's here, all right." Jax started to write again.

And then Jared saw her, her dark hair gleaming
in the summer sunshine as she stepped out of the
carriage. Her shoulders were back, her head held
high—she was exactly as he remembered her.

He wasn't close enough to see the smile that
he knew must be on her beautiful face, and he
began to run, shouting her name as he dodged the
heavy traffic that cluttered the street.

Carrie's head turned, and Jared knew the exact
instant that she saw him. Her eyes opened wide,
her face went pale and her delicate lips moved as
she soundlessly spoke his name.

As he skidded to a stop in front of her, it was
all he could do to keep from pulling her into his
arms and covering her mouth with his own.

"Oh, come on," Jared fumed. "After all this time, you're not going to let me kiss her?"

"Chill out," Jax muttered as he continued to write. "You're not alone."

But Jared was aware of the gentleman and two elderly ladies standing near her, so he reined in his desire and simply smiled at her.

She was more beautiful than ever. Dressed as she was, she looked every inch the proper lady, but Jared saw she still had a spark of fire in her deep blue eyes. It was that spark that had become a flame on the day they had met, the day he had found her riding her father's nearly uncontrollable stallion, dressed in her brother's clothes, in the field above the manor house. She had seemed as wild and untamable as the horse, and he had fallen in love with her instantly.

Jared could feel Carrie's eyes studying him, taking in the expensive cut of his clothes, the leanness of his body, the drawn, thin lines of his face.

"I thought you were dead," she whispered, her low voice husky with emotion.

"You know this man?" the gentleman standing beside her asked. He was several years older than Jared, with a round face and a pair of spectacles that magnified his brown eyes.

Carrie turned to look at him, as if she was startled that he was there. For the briefest of instants, Jared saw what might have been fear in her eyes.

"Yes," she answered slowly, as if she was choosing her words carefully. "Harlan, this is Jared Dexter, an old friend of my family's." She looked back at Jared, and he saw that her eyes were nearly brimming over with unshed tears. ''Jared, I'd like you to meet Harlan Kent. My husband.''

It was easy to write Jared's reaction to the news that Carrie had married another man. Jax knew firsthand about the waves of disbelief, anger and pure heart-breaking sorrow that swept over Jared. He knew about the misery and could describe the sensations in absolute vivid detail.

With a few quick sentences, he brought Jared back to the privacy of his fancy hotel room, where his hero put his head down and cried.

Just the way Jax had done when he realized that Kelly would not be his, that he had come home too late.

Chapter 5

Dear Kelly,
August 24. Your eighteenth birthday.

I spend the day thinking about you. I remember how you invited me to spend your thirteenth birthday with you. We went downtown to the aquarium and looked in the top of the big fish tank. We stared at the skeletons of sharks hanging from the ceiling, sharks big enough to eat us both for breakfast and still go hungry.

For the first time in the three months I have been here, I cry.

Worse than the black eyes and the bruises and cuts and broken ribs, worse than the fear that today may be the day they drag me out of my cell and kill me, worse than the insults and the degradation, the filth and the stench, worse than all that, they have made me break my promise

to you. That fills me with pain so great that I
can't stop the tears.

I try to imagine your day, where you go, what
you do.

Do you wonder where I am? Do you expect
me at least to call?

Right now I'd sell my soul to the devil for a
telephone.

I wonder if anyone even knows where I am.

The warden laughs and hits me when I ask,
then tells me the government has told my London magazine that I died in a cholera epidemic.

But, Kelly, I am not dead.

You come to me tonight, eighteen years old
and so lovely. Your eyes are so sad. We hold
each other tightly, and I fall asleep with you in
my arms.

But when I wake up, you are gone.

I love you.

Love, T.

Friday morning dawned gray and rainy. Kelly worked
on her novel straight through until the early afternoon,
grabbing a peanut butter and jelly sandwich on her
way to get dressed to go to the university lecture series.

Normally the dismal weather would have kept her
inside, but today's guest speaker was none other than
Jayne Tyler, one of the hottest names in women's fiction. Tyler had rocketed onto the *New York Times*
bestseller list with her first novel three years ago, and
since then she had written five books, each one better
than the last. She created hot, spicy characters that
seemed to leap off the pages, and stories full of in-
trigue and passion. She could have her reader laughing

on one page and reaching for a tissue to dry her tears on the next. And Tyler really knew what romance was. She knew exactly the right amount of gentle tenderness to throw in to cut straight through to the reader's heart.

Today she was going to speak in front of a roomful of hopeful authors and fans, spilling her secrets. And Kelly was going to be there, paying close attention.

She dressed carefully in her favorite dress, a beige-and-tan-checked shirtdress with a flared, nearly floor-length skirt, and long sleeves that she rolled up casually to her elbows.

The rawness of the rainy day penetrated her apartment, and there was a decided draft up the full skirt. So Kelly pulled a pair of slim black leggings on underneath the skirt. Still feeling cold, she unbuttoned the dress down to her waist and slipped a tank-style undershirt on, then put her arms back into the sleeves. She adjusted the small shoulder pads and rebuttoned the dress. With her black cowboy boots on her feet, a wide leather belt around her waist, her hair back in a casual ponytail, and silver earrings with shiny black stones dangling from her ears, she was ready to go.

Amazingly, the trolley was running ahead of schedule, and as she disembarked, she put up her umbrella against the drizzle and glanced at her watch. She was nearly two hours early. She rolled her eyes. Just a tad overeager. Still, if she had timed it perfectly, the trolley would have broken down and she would have ended up being two hours late.

She eyed the row of shops across from the campus lecture hall as she pulled her denim jacket more tightly around her. Somewhere over there was a shop called Quick Cuts, and Marcy had recommended it soundly the last time Kelly had made noise about getting her hair cut.

She hesitated only a few seconds, then made her way across the street, dodging the puddles as she went.

Jax glanced at the clock on the dashboard of his sports car. They were running late because of this damned rain. Bostonians were notorious for their wild driving skills, and add a little rain to the equation—the end result was sheer chaos.

His sister, Stefanie, was sitting next to him, calmly filing her fingernails.

"There's no way I'm going to find a parking spot," he told her. "I'm going to have to drop you."

"Oh, no, you're not." She put her emery board into her purse and looked up at him. "I'm *not* going in there alone, Jax. We'll both be late together."

"Stef—"

"Relax, darling, they can't start this party without us." Stefanie pulled down the mirror that was part of her sun visor and checked her perfectly styled blond curls. "I'm the guest of honor, remember?"

"I'm not worried about that. I just want to be able to leave on time."

Stefanie's gray eyes were filled with speculation as she looked up from putting on another coat of lipstick. "It's a woman, isn't it?"

Jax kept his face expressionless. He didn't even glance in her direction.

"I *knew* it," she said triumphantly, reattaching the top to the lipstick and tossing it into her purse. "It is, isn't it? You're finally over that girl—what was her name? Kevin's sister. Kelly. The one you wrote that collection of letters to. The one who was so young."

Again Jackson didn't say a word. He just drove the car. They were close enough now to start looking for a parking space.

"You know, your entire affair with her was too dreadfully romantic." Stefanie wouldn't let up. "She was just a teenager, a child really, while you were a grown man. I know forbidden fruit has a rep for being sweeter and all that, but carrying a torch for her all these years borders on the absurd. Not that I don't appreciate the absurd, of course. And it *is* rather disgustingly romantic of you." She watched him carefully. "I was thinking it might be a good story idea for the next contemporary novel—"

Jax turned and glared at her. "No."

"Made you look." She grinned toothily, then laughed at his exasperation. "You're *not* over her, are you? Well, maybe this new woman can sufficiently distract you for a while anyway. Tell me all about her, darling. What's her name? Where'd you meet her— Look, that car's leaving!"

And so it was. Jax braked to a stop behind a small blue Honda that was pulling out of a miniature parking spot. As he wrestled his car into the space that was barely twelve inches bigger than the length of his car, a young woman standing at the crosswalk waiting for the light to change caught his eye. Something about the way she was standing looked familiar. He caught a glimpse of short, sleek, dark hair underneath her umbrella as she turned away.

As he pulled up the parking brake and cut the engine, Jax watched a transit bus speed past. It sent a sheet of muddy water into the air. The young woman jumped back, but not quickly enough, and her skirt was drenched.

"Oh, yuck." Stefanie was watching, too. "The poor thing."

Jackson checked his watch. "Stef, we've got to hurry."

But his sister's eyes had widened as she watched the movements of the young woman on the sidewalk. The woman had stepped back, away from the street, and had set down her backpack and umbrella under the awning of an ice cream parlor.

Jax followed Stefanie's gaze, and watched, too, as the woman calmly took off her denim jacket and placed it on the top of her backpack. She took off a wide brown belt, set that on top of her jacket, then began to unbutton her dress.

She pushed off the top of the muddy dress, revealing a black sleeveless tank top and long, slender arms. Feeling rather like a voyeur, Jax made himself look away. But there was something so familiar about her. He looked back to see her pushing the dress down around her thighs. She wore a pair of skintight black leggings on her long legs. She had very, *very* long legs.

"Do try to keep your tongue inside your mouth, Jax darling," Stefanie said dryly.

As Jackson watched, the woman stepped out of her dress, shaking it slightly to get her cowboy boots free—

Cowboy boots!

"She got her hair cut," Jax breathed, and Stefanie looked at him in surprise.

"You know her?"

But Jax was already out of the car.

Kelly folded her muddy dress small enough to fit into her backpack. She wished she could rinse it out, but the lecture was going to start in just a few minutes. She hoped the mud wouldn't stain before she had a chance to go home and wash it clean.

"God," she heard a voice say. "It *is* you."

Startled, she looked up from where she was crouching to see T. Jackson towering above her.

"I love it," he said simply as she slowly stood and faced him. "Your hair—it's great."

She was gorgeous. Dressed all in black, her leggings and tank top hugging every inch of her lithe body, and with her dark hair cut very short—shorter even than his—she looked like a chic New York City model. Her hair capped her head, cut so short in the front that she could barely be described as having bangs. Pointed sideburns of hair hung down in front of each ear, curving in to accentuate the prettiness of her face, framing her big blue eyes. Her hair was buzzed short around her ears and in the back, but the effect was remarkably feminine. Her neck looked long and graceful and very, very vulnerable.

She looked as if she were twelve again. His gaze dropped down to her body. Well, maybe not exactly...

Kelly pulled her jacket on, more as protection from his eyes than from the cold. "You're following me again." It wasn't even a question. "Do us both a favor, Jackson. Give up."

"You know I'm not going to do that," he said softly. "And actually, this time I'm not following you." He looked at his watch again. "I've got to go—"

"Aren't you going to introduce me?"

Kelly turned to see a tall woman standing next to Jax, her hand possessively on his arm. She was strikingly beautiful, tall and slim, with hair like spun gold that shimmered and curled around her face. Her perfect mouth was curved upward in a friendly smile, but her cool gray eyes were inquisitive, curious.

Surprise rushed through her. This had to be Jackson's wife. Funny how he hadn't mentioned he was married...

"Kelly, this is Stefanie Winchester," Jax said. "Stef, meet Kelly O'Brien."

Stefanie *Winchester.* Oh, Lord, she *was* his wife. The wave of jealousy that shot through Kelly shocked her. No, it couldn't be jealousy she was feeling. Maybe it was indigestion—something she ate. As she shook the cool, slim hand that Stefanie extended, Kelly missed the pointed look of surprise and interest that the blond woman sent Jax.

"My brother's told me so much about you," Stefanie said, her voice cool and cultured.

Brother?

Stefanie was T. Jackson's *sister,* not his wife. Of course. Stefanie. *Stef.* Jax had told her about his older sister, Stef.

Kelly looked up to find Jax's eyes on her. He was watching her steadily, and he smiled very slightly, as if he knew what she was thinking. But he glanced at his watch again and turned to his sister.

"We're late." He looked back at Kelly. "I'll see you later."

She shook her head and opened her mouth to protest, but he stopped her by cupping her face with one hand and pressing his thumb lightly against her lips.

"I *will* see you later," he said, his voice soft and so dangerously positive. "You *are* going to have dinner with me and we *are* going to talk. Tonight."

Kelly couldn't move as she gazed into his eyes. He

was looking at her with an intensity that was hypnotizing. As she watched, his gaze dropped to her mouth, and she knew with a flash of heat that he was going to kiss her.

But he didn't.

Instead he brushed his thumb lightly against her lips, letting his fingers linger before he turned to leave. He walked backward all the way to the curb, a smile spreading across his handsome face.

"You *do* look..." He shook his head, as if unable to find the words. "Wonderfully," he finally said, "amazingly, fabulously, unbelievably, deliciously—"

"You could probably stand to insert an adjective right about now," Stefanie said dryly.

"Sexy," he whispered, but his voice carried quite clearly to Kelly.

"I'll be over about eight," he said.

"No." Kelly finally found her voice, but it was too late. He'd already turned and was halfway across the street.

With a sigh of frustration, she picked up her backpack and her umbrella and went back to the curb, where the Don't Walk sign was flashing. She waited far from the puddles for the light to change.

"Kelly, huh?" Stefanie said, giving Jax a sidelong glance as they went into the university building. "So it's still little Kelly O'Brien that you've got it bad for, even after all these years. Although she's not so little anymore, is she?"

"No, she's not," Jax agreed.

"I thought she got married."

"She did. It didn't work out."

"Lucky you," Stefanie said. "So naturally you've

got your catcher's mitt on, ready to grab her on the rebound.''

"You're mixing your sports metaphors," Jackson countered, not commenting on the truth of what she'd just said.

"And *you're* going for the big, happy Hollywood ending," Stefanie decided. "You *are* a hopeless romantic, aren't you, darling?"

"Everything I've ever written has a happy ending," Jax told his sister. "It shouldn't be *too* hard to orchestrate a real one for my life."

"I hope so." In an unusual display of affection, Stefanie reached out and squeezed Jax's hand. "But you know, real people aren't as easy to manipulate as fictional characters."

Jackson's smile turned rueful. "You're telling me. And lately my fictional characters haven't been easy to manipulate, either."

Dear Kelly,
I have finished.

True, it's only a rough draft, but what more do you want for a first novel written in pencil between the printed lines of a paperback called *Passion's Destiny?*

It's a romance. Why? I needed to write a book with a happy ending, and since I've read nothing but these three romance novels in the past eleven months, I figured it was a good place to start.

And I promise in the next draft I'll change my heroine's first name from Kelly. She is you, though—beautiful and strong and proud.

I read my book over and over. Reading between the lines suddenly has a real meaning for me.

It has been nearly a year.

I pray that someday, somehow I will see you again. I live for that day.

I love you.

Love, T.

Chapter 6

Kelly went into the crowded lecture hall, scanning the auditorium for an empty seat. As usual, there were chairs free in the front, so she went down the sloped aisle and sat down in the second row on the end.

It wasn't too long before the representative from the college lecture series came out onto the stage and, after testing the microphone, introduced bestselling author Jayne Tyler.

Kelly joined the enthusiastic applause, but then stopped suddenly, staring in disbelief at the woman who had walked out and now stood behind the podium.

It was Stefanie Winchester.

T. Jackson's sister was Jayne Tyler?

Why not? thought Kelly, laughing to herself at the irony. She knew Tyler was a pen name.

She spotted T. leaning lazily against the wall in the front of the lecture hall, his arms casually crossed. He was looking out over the audience, occasionally glancing up at the stage, at his sister.

But then his eyes met hers. He straightened up, staring at her, frowning slightly as if he couldn't figure out what Kelly was doing here.

She heard Stefanie introduce herself and her brother and agent, Jackson.

Brother and...

Agent?

Kelly looked back at T. Jackson. His gaze was fixed on her, and he smiled slightly.

Jackson wondered what Kelly was doing here, as she gave her full attention to his sister. He glanced at his watch. Stef's speech would take another forty minutes, then there'd be a question-and-answer period, during which he'd make an attempt to take control. Stef didn't like answering questions, and he couldn't blame her. People tended to ask the damnedest things.

He glanced up at his sister. She looked calm and collected, and her speech had been well rehearsed. She was doing fine. He stopped paying attention to Stef's words. He'd heard this speech too many times; hell, he'd written the damned thing.

He let his eyes drift back to Kelly. She hadn't put up a fight today when he'd told her he was taking her to dinner.

He wanted to hold her in his arms tonight. Quickly he ran down a mental list of posh Boston restaurants, trying to remember which places had a band and a dance floor. The last time he'd danced with Kelly, she had felt so good in his arms, and they'd both been so optimistic about the future....

The junior prom had been held in the high school

gym. The lights had been down low, and the room had been decorated with crepe streamers and helium balloons. It had looked about as romantic as a badly decorated gymnasium could be, but Jax hadn't cared. Just holding Kelly in his arms had been nearly an overload of romance.

From the number of curious stares he and Kelly were getting, Jackson knew he was the object of much discussion among both the other students and the teachers. It was obvious that he was much older than Kelly.

He wanted to pull her close, closer than he was holding her, but he was afraid to. He was afraid of attracting even more attention. But most of all, he was afraid of what people would think. Not about him—he didn't care about himself. But he *did* care about Kelly, and he was afraid people would assume that since he was dating her, she must be sleeping with him.

She still had another year to go in this school, with these kids. It wouldn't be easy for her if she were labeled, tagged with that kind of reputation.

Jax looked down to see her smiling up at him. He smiled back, but concern instantly darkened her eyes.

"What's wrong?" she asked.

He laughed, shaking his head. "I can't hide anything from you, can I?"

Her fingers were twisted in the hair that went down over the back of his collar. She shifted her weight so that her body brushed against his. He could feel her long, firm thighs against his, the softness of her breasts against his chest. It felt like heaven, but he had to make her stop.

"Kel," he said, unsure how to explain. "Have you noticed the amount of attention we're getting?"

She glanced around the room, then smiled back at Jax. "I think it's because you're the most handsome man here."

"The key word is *man*." Jax took a deep breath. He had to just say it. "Kelly, I'm afraid if we dance too close, people are going to think we're…involved."

"We *are* involved." She watched him steadily. "Aren't we?"

He gazed into her lovely face for several long moments. She was so beautiful, so mature in so many ways, yet still such an innocent. "I meant… *intimately* involved."

A tinge of pink crept across her cheeks, but she didn't look away from him. "I don't care what other people think about me."

"But I do," he said softly. "I care very much. Once people give someone a label, it's almost impossible to change it. Trust me, I'm speaking from experience."

Kelly didn't say anything. She simply gazed up at him, waiting for him to go on.

"You know that I graduated from public high school out on Cape Cod," he told her. "Out in Dennis."

She nodded.

"I only went to that school for the end of my junior year and my senior year," he explained. "Before that, I went to prep school. Lots of different prep schools."

"I didn't know that."

Jax moved with her across the dance floor to the slow rock ballad. Every few minutes he had to remind himself to loosen his hold on her, because every few minutes he forgot his resolve and his arm tightened around her waist, drawing her closer to him. "Yeah." He had to clear his throat. "By the end of my junior year, I'd been kicked out of so many prep schools, there weren't any left that would accept me."

"Kicked out?" Kelly was surprised. "You?"

He released her to point to the tiny scar on his left cheekbone. "Remember that fight I was in?" He put his arm back around her. "Well, I won the fight, but I got booted out of school. And *that* didn't win me any points with the folks," he added with a grin.

"You never told me what you fought about."

"Freshman hazing. The seniors were merciless. I watched one kid after another get hurt by their supposedly harmless pranks, and when they went too far, I...um, went a little crazy."

"What did they do?"

Jackson grimaced. "They put something in the food and made the entire freshman class really sick. I was late to lunch that day, and when I walked into the mess hall and saw all the seniors standing around laughing at all the freshmen—and some of them were *violently* sick—I got upset. When I found out who had masterminded the scheme, I broke his nose." He shrugged. "Apparently making fifty kids blow groceries is good clean fun, whereas breaking a senior's nose is not."

The band segued directly into another slow, pulsating song. Jax could feel perspiration forming on his forehead as Kelly rested her head on his shoulder. He wanted to kiss her, he wanted to hold her tightly, feel the length of her slim, soft body against his. But she was only sixteen. It was good that they were here, with all these people watching. If there ever were a time he needed a chaperone, it was right now.

But even after tonight, he'd have to endure a year

and a half of wanting something he couldn't have. He looked down into Kelly's eyes and he was overcome by a rush of emotions. He loved her, and he wanted to be near her all the time. Sex only played a very small part in the way he felt about her—

Who was he kidding? He would come damn close to selling his soul for a chance to make love to her. It wouldn't be easy to live through the next few years. In fact, if Kelly managed to remain a virgin until she was eighteen, they would both deserve sainthood.

"That was the first prep school," Kelly said, breaking into his thoughts. "Why were you kicked out of the others?"

"I kept getting kicked out because I went in with a bad reputation," Jax told her. "At the second school, I was in the wrong place at the wrong time. Someone set fire to the athletic supply shed, and because I came in pegged as a troublemaker, I ended up taking the blame. By the time I was a junior, I was at my fifth boarding school. I went in on probation, and managed to get asked to leave simply because I dropped my tray in the dining hall one morning."

"That's awful."

"It happens. Once you're labeled, it's all over." He shook his head. "I don't want that to happen to you, Kel."

"T., somehow I don't think my connection to you is going to hurt my reputation." Kelly laughed. "It just might help it, if you want to know the truth."

Jax looked down into her sparkling eyes, feeling his heart expanding in his chest. He loved her. Good God, he'd loved her for years, but he'd refused to admit it, even to himself, because she had been only a child. All that time, he'd wondered what was wrong with him, why he never dated any of the women at school for more than a week or two. He'd led himself to believe that he was simply not cut out for long-term relationships, that one woman simply didn't have the ability to hold his attention for very long. He'd come to the conclusion that marriage and a family were simply not in his future.

But the real truth was, he was more monogamous than most men his age. Kelly owned his heart and soul, had owned it for years. Jax knew without a shadow of a doubt that he was going to love her until the day he died.

She reached up and touched the side of his face, catching a bead of perspiration that threatened to drip down past his ear. "It's warm in here," she said, her low voice husky.

"Yes," Jackson agreed, his eyes never leaving her face. "It is."

In silent agreement, he led Kelly off the dance floor and out of the gym. The air in the lobby was much cooler, and they moved toward the refreshment table.

"Want a soda?" Jax asked and Kelly nodded.

"Thanks. I've got to go, um… What's the correct euphemism?" She smiled. "Powder my nose? That's as obsolete as dialing a phone, isn't it? I'll meet you out here."

She pulled away from him, but Jax didn't let go of her fingers until the last possible moment. He watched her walk down the hallway. She was elegant and poised, full of the self-confidence that made her so unique among her peers. The heels she wore on her feet made her hips sway slightly as she went, and he didn't look away until the girls' room door closed behind her.

But then he turned and came face-to-face with an older man who had silently moved to stand at his side.

"Kelly looks lovely tonight," the man, obviously one of the teachers, said. He was smiling at Jax, but that smile didn't reach his eyes. "I didn't realize she was dating a college...boy."

It was obvious to Jax that this teacher didn't consider him a boy at all.

But he returned the smile, holding out his hand. "I'm Jackson Winchester," he said easily. "I've been a friend of Kelly's for some time now."

"Ted Henderson. What school are you going to?"

"I went to Boston College," Jax replied.

"Went?" Henderson's cold brown eyes probed for more information.

"I've graduated," Jax explained.

"You're *out* of college." Henderson made sure he got it straight. "Isn't Kelly a little bit young for you?"

"I don't see how that's any business of yours, Ted." Jax spoke pleasantly, but the older man's eyes darkened with disapproval anyway.

"I care about Kelly." Henderson crossed his arms in front of him, all pretense at pleasantness dropped. "I'm a friend of her father's—"

"Nolan approves of my relationship with his daughter." Jax didn't know if that was *exactly* the truth, but Nolan O'Brien wouldn't have let him take Kelly to the prom in the first place if he didn't want them to date, would he have?

"If that's the case," Henderson countered, "then I truly doubt that he's seen the way you look at that girl." He shook his head. "You're a grown man, Winchester. She's only a child. You have no right to take the rest of her childhood away from her."

Jax kept his face carefully neutral, taking out his wallet as he turned past the teacher and headed toward the refreshment table. But Henderson followed.

"Kelly should be involved with boys her own age," he persisted. "She should be having lighthearted romances, she should be having fun. I'm sure she's flattered by the attention you give her—what young girl wouldn't be? I'm sure you don't need to be reminded about your good looks."

Jackson paid for two cans of soda, then turned back to Henderson. "Have you finished?"

"Just about." Henderson blocked Jax's way with his bulk, pinning the younger man against the refreshment table. "I just want to make sure you're aware of the laws in Massachusetts regarding statutory rape—"

"I don't need any lectures, Ted." Jax forced himself to speak slowly, without any trace of his anger evident in his voice. "Like you said, I'm a grown man. I'm well aware of any consequences my actions might bring. But I love Kelly, and I believe that she loves me. Now, if you'll excuse me?"

"I don't doubt that you love her, son," Henderson said, his voice surprisingly gentle. "But she's only sixteen. You don't really expect whatever she feels for you will last, do you?"

Jax saw Kelly come out of the bathroom and start down the hall toward him. "Yes," he said shortly to Henderson, nearly pushing past him. "I do. Excuse me."

He walked toward Kelly, watching her face break into a beautiful smile as she saw him. He watched her eyes dance with pleasure, watched her dress cling to her body as she moved. But Ted Henderson's quiet voice trailed after him. "High school should be a carefree, happy time. Your relationship with Kelly can only be a burden, Winchester. If you really love the girl, you won't do that to her.''

Jax opened one of the cans of soda and handed it to Kelly when they met farther down the hallway. ''They didn't have any cups,'' he apologized. ''I wiped off the top for you.''

''Thanks,'' she murmured, taking a sip of the soda.

He led her back into the dimness of the gym, where they found an empty table off to the side of the dance floor and sat down. He could feel Kelly watching him as he opened his own can of soda and took a long drink.

''You're not having much fun, are you?'' she asked softly.

''I'm having a great time—''

''Someone in the girls' room told me that Mr. Henderson was giving you the third degree, telling you how wrong it was for us to be here together.'' She leaned toward him. ''That doesn't sound like a great time to me. We can leave, T. I won't mind if you want to go—''

''Are you kidding? I want to dance with you some more.''

Kelly covered his hand with hers, gently lacing their fingers together. ''We could go somewhere else and…dance.''

Jax felt a hot flare of desire shoot through him as he met her steady gaze. She wasn't talking about dancing. She was talking about… He swallowed.

Sixteen, he reminded himself. She was only sixteen.

''I think we'd better stay here,'' he said quietly.

''Are you sure?''

Jax laughed desperately. ''Kelly, come on. I need

you to help me out, not make things harder than they already are.'' As soon as the words were out of his mouth, he realized just how full of sexual innuendo they were. To his relief, Kelly didn't seem to notice.

''While I was in the girls' room, I heard a little of the gossip that's going around about you and me,'' Kelly said. ''And you were right. I *have* been relabeled.''

''Oh, no.'' Jax frowned with concern. ''Not already—''

But Kelly was smiling, her blue eyes shining with delight. ''They're calling me…a studcatcher.'' She laughed. ''You, of course, being the stud in question. It's a big step up for me from my last label.''

''Which was…?''

''Math nerd.'' Kelly made a face. ''Hardly flattering and particularly galling since I'm planning to major in language arts when I go to college. I like studcatcher much better.'' She grinned. ''Wanna dance with me, stud?''

Jax feigned indignation as he followed her onto the dance floor and took her into his arms. ''Is that all I am to you? Just a stud?''

Her smile softened and her eyes grew warm as she tipped her head back to look up at him. ''Tyrone, I fell in love with you before I knew what a stud was.''

I fell in love with you….

Her words echoed over and over in Jax's head. She loved him. She loved him!

''Oh, Kel,'' he breathed.

Both of her arms had been around his neck, and she'd pulled his head down to her waiting lips.

He'd kissed her. Right there in the middle of the dance floor. A slow, soft, lingering kiss…

The sound of three hundred pairs of hands clapping startled Jax out of his reverie. The crowd of people in the university auditorium was applauding. Stefanie's speech was over.

Momentarily off balance, he looked for Kelly. It had grown warm in the room, and she had taken off her denim jacket. God, in that outfit she looked good enough to eat.

As if she could feel his eyes on her, she glanced in his direction.

T. Jackson was staring at her with that same hungry look in his eyes. He *wasn't* going to give up, Kelly realized with a flare of despair. He wasn't going to quit until they gave in to the desire that still burned between them, until they finally made love.

But maybe that was the answer. Kelly watched as he climbed the stairs to the stage and crossed to stand next to his sister. His blond hair glistened in the stage lights, and his teeth flashed as he smiled. He took over the podium from Stefanie, introducing the question-and-answer portion of the program. He spoke easily, confidently, his wonderful charisma set to full power as he fielded questions from the floor.

Making love to T. would probably be pretty damn good.

Kelly gazed at the wide expanse of his shoulders. His muscular arms were covered by the sleeves of his well-tailored tweed jacket, arms that led down to a pair of strong, long-fingered hands that now gripped the sides of the podium. What would it feel like to have those hands touch her body?

It was a rhetorical question, but Kelly's imagination took over, producing a vivid picture of T., naked in her bed, with fire in his eyes as he touched her, kissed her, made love to her— She shook her head, forcing herself to pay attention to the questions that were being asked.

"What's your writing schedule like?" a woman in the back of the lecture hall asked.

"Jayne usually gets up pretty early in the morning," T. answered, "and crawls straight from her bed to her personal computer, stopping on the way for a cup of coffee. She starts the day by reviewing and revising her previous day's work, then writes until a little before noon. She eats lunch in front of the computer, then about an hour later, takes about a two-hour break—runs on the beach, goes for a swim. After that, she writes until dinner, and usually again after dinner."

"It's pretty intense," Stefanie interjected. "But this way a book can be completed quickly. After it's all over, I take some time off, head for Club Med."

As people raised their hands, hoping to ask another question, Kelly lifted her own hand into the air.

Jax focused on her immediately. "Yeah, Kelly."

She cleared her throat, raising her voice so her question could be heard throughout the huge room. "What do you do when you've got a manuscript that doesn't work, but you can't figure out how to make it better?"

He stared at her, a curious look on his face. "Have you written a book?"

She nodded.

"You never told me that," he said, his voice sounding soft and intimate, even over the PA system.

"You never asked," she countered. She could feel the curious eyes of the audience studying her as she had what was essentially a private conversation in front of them all.

As if he realized this, Jax shifted his weight, looking out at the sea of faces. "Well, there are a couple of solutions," he said. "The first is to put that manuscript on a shelf and start something new. After you finish your next project, you can go back to the problem manuscript and look at it with a new perspective." His eyes found Kelly's face again. "The other solution is to find a critique partner. Work with another person, get another opinion. What may seem an insurmountable problem to you might be a quick fix for someone else." His eyes seemed to sparkle as he shot her his infectious grin. "Next question?"

Jax spent another twenty minutes answering questions, and then the program was over. He waited impatiently as the head of the lecture series shook his hand and long-windedly thanked him and Stefanie for being able to do the program for only a small honorarium.

He could see Kelly walking slowly toward the back doors of the lecture hall, talking to another young woman—Marcy something from the newspaper office. Marcy touched Kelly's hair and walked in a full circle around her. Kelly said something, and the two women broke up. Kelly's musical laugh cut through the ambient noise of the big room like a knife to his heart.

He turned to the lecture series head and skillfully interrupted her. "I'm so sorry," he apologized, "but we've really got to go. Jayne's got another appointment and—"

"Oh, yes, of course," the woman said. "So nice to have met you, and thanks again."

Grabbing Stefanie's arm with one hand and snatch-

ing up her coat and purse with his other, he dragged
her down toward the main entrance of the hall.

Marcy was gone, but Kelly stood in the lobby, putting on her backpack. The light drizzle had turned into
a heavy rain that fell like a sheet of water outside the
open door. About to put her umbrella up, Kelly was
ready to plunge into the downpour.

"Kel, wait!"

Kelly turned back to see T. striding toward her.

"Let me give you a ride home," he said. "You
don't really want to stand in this, waiting for a trolley,
do you?"

He wasn't really standing that close, but it seemed
as if she could feel the heat from his body. Again,
unbidden, the image of their naked bodies, intertwined
as they made love, appeared in her head. Only, this
time, the sound of rain on the roof and the duskiness
of gray, late-afternoon light coming in through her
bedroom windows completed the vision.

Oh, how she wanted him.

It was nothing but animal attraction. Lust. It was
the remnants of years of fantasy. If only she could
wipe those feelings from her memory, wash him out
of her system.

Maybe she could....

Making love to T. Jackson couldn't possibly be as
good as she imagined. But there was only one way to
prove that, and that was to make love to him. By making love to him, she would satisfy both her curiosity
and her desire, and prove that he was nothing special
to her, not anymore.

He, too, would get what he wanted, and then maybe
he would leave her alone.

"All right," she heard herself say, and saw the surprise in his eyes. He'd been expecting a fight.

"I'll pull the car around," he said, as if he were afraid that if he didn't act fast, she'd change her mind. "Wait here with Stef, okay?" With a quick smile, he was gone.

Kelly turned to find his sister watching her.

"I had no idea you were Jayne Tyler," Kelly said. "I've really enjoyed your books."

Stephanie shrugged almost nonchalantly. "Thanks."

"Is Jackson doing any writing these days?" Kelly asked. "That was always his dream."

"You *do* care about him." The older woman watched Kelly closely. "Don't you?"

It was Kelly's turn to shrug as she looked out the door at the street, watching for Jax's car. "Well, yeah. He was my best friend for years. I'll always care about him."

"Why did you marry that other man?"

Kelly looked up, surprised at the personal nature of the question, surprised that Stefanie even knew she'd been married.

Jax's car pulled up to the curb, saving Kelly from having to answer. "Come on, you can share my umbrella," she said instead, and the two women dashed out into the rain.

Stefanie got into the tiny back seat, so Kelly took the front, shaking her umbrella rather futilely as she closed it and pulled it into the car behind her.

The shoulders of T.'s jacket were soaked, and drops of water dripped from his wet hair onto his face. "I'm going to take Stefanie to the hotel," he said. "And if you don't mind, I'd like to change before we go out to dinner. We *are* going out to dinner, remember?"

"I'm not exactly dressed for anything fancy, T.,'' Kelly protested. "I don't want to—''

"I didn't mean fancy,'' he interrupted. "I meant *dry.* I stepped into a puddle, and my sock is wet.'' He grinned. "I *knew* there was a reason I don't wear socks.''

Kelly had to smile. "And here, all this time, I thought you just didn't like to do the extra laundry.''

He put the car into gear, signaling to move out into the steady stream of traffic. "If you want, we can get something to eat right at the hotel.''

As T. Jackson headed toward downtown Boston on Commonwealth Avenue, Kelly settled back into the comfortable leather seat of his car. She looked out the window, through the drops of rain, and let her mind wander to the last time she'd been in a car with this man....

Chapter 7

It was nearly 5:00 a.m., and T. Jackson and Kelly were parked at the beach. After the lights and glare of three different after-prom parties, the intimate quiet of the predawn was wonderful.

They'd left the last party several hours early, and now they sat quietly talking and holding hands.

T. told her about his dream of becoming a writer. He wanted to write everything—novels, short stories, screenplays. He wanted to write comedies most of all, stories with happy endings.

He talked about growing up, about his family, his parents. They loved him, he'd told her, but they just didn't know how to show it. When T. had been kicked out of the last prep school that would accept him, his mother had been in Milan, and his father had been on a three-month cruise in the South Pacific. He'd talked to each of them on the telephone, and they both said the same thing—military school.

"So I told my mother that Dad was going to take care of everything, and I told my dad that my mother was making all of the arrangements, and I packed up my things and drove out to the summer house we had on the Cape." His voice was smooth and soft in the darkness. "I took a couple days off, did errands, restocked the house with food." He laughed softly. "Thank God for credit cards. Then I forged a letter from my parents and went over to the high school and registered. I had a copy of my school records, and I weeded out all the mention of disciplinary action. I left out anything that said I'd been expelled. I entered the school almost anonymously, and I kept a low profile and did okay."

"You lived by yourself?" She couldn't see his expression in the darkness, not until he smiled.

"Yeah. It was tough getting around those parent-teacher conferences, though."

"But your parents must've known—"

"Not until Christmas break during my senior year," he said. "By that time, I was almost eighteen, and they figured I had things under control."

"Weren't you lonely?" she asked softly.

T. was very quiet. "I didn't know what I was missing," he admitted. "Not until I met your family. Not until I met you."

Kelly could see that he was watching her, and she felt his hand touch the side of her face, felt his lips brush hers. She heard him make a low sound, a groan, as he pulled away.

"Kel, we should go home." His voice was raspy.

Her heart was pounding in her chest, making her feel as if she were about to explode. "Please, T., let's not go yet. Let's take a walk on the beach."

Even as she spoke, she slipped off her shoes and rolled down her stockings.

Outside the car, the night air was cold. In the east, the sky was starting to lighten. It wouldn't be long before the sun came up. Kelly turned to see T. standing almost uncertainly by the car. She took his hand and pulled, leading him out onto the soft sand.

"Wait a sec," he said, reaching down to pull off his own shoes and socks. He left them in a pile next to his car.

As they walked along the edge of the water, T. Jackson draped his jacket around her shoulders and held her close to him for added warmth. The water was icy as it occasionally splashed up onto their bare feet, but Kelly didn't care.

She was in heaven.

"I don't want tonight to end," she whispered.

T. stopped walking, turning her to face him, pulling her in even closer to him. "I don't want it to, either."

He kissed her then, and she could feel his restraint. He was holding so much back. She pressed herself against the hard muscles of his chest and, feeling shockingly bold, she opened her mouth underneath his and touched his lips with her tongue.

She heard him groan and felt his arms tighten around her as he parted his lips under her gentle pressure. His mouth tasted wonderful, so moist and warm and soft.

She could feel his control slipping as he returned her kisses. Each kiss was longer, deeper, more passionate than the last. His hands moved across her body, and his jacket fell off her shoulders onto the sand.

One of his legs pressed between hers as they both

tried to get closer, even closer, to each other. She could feel his hands in her hair, pulling out the pins, letting it hang down around her shoulders.

He found the slit in the back of her dress, and the sensation of his fingers on her bare skin made Kelly cry out.

He pulled back then, breathing hard. She could feel his heart pumping in his chest, echoing the crazy beat of her own heart.

"God, Kelly—"

She pulled his head down, pulled his lips to her and kissed him again. He resisted for all of half a second, then nearly crushed her mouth with his as his careful control slipped even further. Kelly felt an additional flash of pleasure, an even stronger flash of heat that seemed to spread throughout her entire body as she realized the power she had over him.

"Jackson, make love to me."

Her words made him freeze, until she began kissing his chin, his neck, instinctively pressing the soft place between her legs against the solid muscles of his thigh. That seemed to drive him crazy, and he kissed her, a savage kiss that made all of his other kisses seem tame in comparison. Together they lost their balance, falling backward onto the soft sand.

And still he kissed her.

She wrapped her arms around T.'s neck, feeling his weight on top of her. His hands swept her body, touching her in ways that left her breathless and wanting more. She felt his hand move up the long, smooth length of her thigh, pushing her skirt up, freeing her legs so that he could lie between them—

That was when Kevin showed up at the beach, looking for them.

That was when her wonderful night with Jackson turned into a nightmare.

Kevin was incensed, pulling Jax off of her. "You promised me!" he shouted. "You gave me your word, you son of a bitch—"

The sky was light in the east, and the first rays of the sun shot up, over the edge of the horizon.

Kelly could see T.'s face in the pale light, and his eyes looked frantic, shocked, as he scrambled to his feet.

"Oh, God, what was I doing?" he gasped. "Kevin, man, I didn't mean to—"

Kevin charged him, but T. didn't make a move to defend himself. "No!" Kelly cried out as her brother's big fist slammed into T. Jackson's face.

T. reeled backward as Kevin hit him again and again.

"You bastard," Kevin kept saying. "You *bastard*—"

"Stop it!" Kelly sobbed, throwing herself onto Kevin's back, trying to hold his arms, trying to keep him from hitting T. again.

Jackson hit the ground, blood dripping from his nose and split lip. He pushed himself up onto his hands and knees until a well-aimed kick from Kevin sent him back down onto the sand.

Kelly threw herself down next to Jax. His face was bleeding, and he held his side as if one of his ribs had been cracked. "Oh, T., I'm sorry," she cried.

"Kelly, are you all right?" he asked, his green eyes trying to focus on her face. "I didn't hurt you, did I? I'm so sorry, what was I *do*ing?"

She shrieked, startled, as her brother roughly hauled

her to her feet. "You stay away from him," he ordered her. "I oughta knock some sense into *you,* too."

He pulled his arm back, as if he was going to slap her the way he had so many times when they were both children. Instinctively Kelly flinched, but then was nearly knocked over as T. suddenly lunged at Kevin.

Almost effortlessly, he took Kevin down. Before she could blink, her brother lay with his face in the sand, Jackson straddling him. T. had Kevin's arm tightly, savagely twisted behind his back, and he pushed it up until her brother cried out with pain.

"You *ever* hit her, it'll be the last thing you do," T. hissed. "Do you understand?"

"Yes," Kevin yelped. "Yes!"

Abruptly T. released Kevin, and they both sat in the sand, catching their breath.

Kevin looked up at Kelly. "Go wait in my car."

"No," she said, wiping the tears from her face. "No, Kevin, I'm going home with Jackson."

There was still a flash of anger in her brother's eyes as he looked up at her. "Jax isn't welcome in our house anymore." He turned to T. "I'll ship your things out to the Cape."

Slowly T. nodded.

Kelly couldn't believe it. He was going to give up, just like that?

"You were supposed to be doing me a favor," Kevin continued, accusingly.

Kelly froze.

"You were helping me out, taking Kelly to the prom, so I could go out with Beth," Kevin said, anger still tingeing his voice. "You *promised* me you wouldn't touch her, you dirtwad."

Jackson had only taken her out as a favor to her brother? Kelly felt sick. He had implied that he loved her, practically proposed marriage to her. But he'd never said the words. He never actually told her that he loved her. But she knew that he did. She *knew* it.

"T.," she started.

"Kelly, go get in my car," Kevin said again.

"Go on, Kel," T. said softly. "I'll call you later."

Numbly she'd walked back to the beach parking lot. Numbly she'd waited for ten, fifteen, twenty minutes until Kevin got into his car beside her and silently drove her home. Numbly she'd climbed the stairs up to her bedroom, peeled off her dress and fallen into bed. But she hadn't slept. She'd waited hours and hours for T. Jackson to call her.

But he never had.

He'd never called, he'd never shown up for their movie date or any of the other many dates they'd planned....

As Jackson pulled his sports car up to the valet at the hotel, Kelly still stared out the window. She'd only seen T. once between prom night and the afternoon last week when he'd shown up at the newspaper office—at Kevin's wedding, when she was nineteen.

Kelly looked up in surprise as T. opened the passenger side door, offering her his hand to help her out. She took his warm fingers lightly, afraid to touch him, but more afraid that if she didn't touch him, he'd realize why.

All his promises had been empty. He had done nothing but let her down ever since prom night. So why in God's name was she still so damned attracted to him?

Because attraction had nothing to do with love.

Love hinged on trust, not on broken promises. But hormones—now, that was an entirely different matter. Kelly's hormones didn't care that T. Jackson hadn't proved to be especially honor-bound. Her hormones only saw a tall, blond, handsome man with a killer smile and a body to die for.

"It was nice meeting you, Kelly." Stefanie interrupted her thoughts. "You should come out to the Cape and visit us sometime this summer."

"Gee, what a swell idea." Jax grinned as he helped Kelly into the hotel. "Why didn't *I* think of that?"

"Thanks, Stefanie." Kelly ignored Jackson. "It was nice meeting you, too. And I really *do* enjoy your books."

"Gotta fly," Stef said. "Emilio's waiting for me." She smiled at Jax. "See you when I see you, darling."

With a flash of blond hair and long legs, she disappeared, leaving Jax and Kelly standing in the posh hotel lobby.

"If you don't mind, I *would* like to change," Jax said.

He began walking toward the elevators, past the entrance to a lounge. To his surprise, Kelly went with him, rather than offering to wait for him in the bar.

"This is a nice place," she said, looking around at the elegantly decorated, airy lobby. The colors were muted shades of pink and rose, with a green-leaf print thrown in for good measure. It was all very soothing and quiet, with thick carpeting and overstuffed furniture to help absorb any excess noise. "I've never been in here."

Jax pushed the up button, and as they stood waiting for the elevator, he watched Kelly. Had she really relaxed enough around him to be comfortable waiting in his suite while he changed his clothes? But she didn't seem relaxed. She seemed quiet, thoughtful almost to the point of distraction.

"What are you thinking about?" he asked.

Her eyes focused on his face. "I was thinking that it's a shame you don't write anymore."

Jax smiled. "Well, I do a little bit here and there."

"But it's not what you do for a living," she said.

The bell rang for the elevator, and Jax held the door open so that she could step inside. As the door slid shut behind him, he pushed the button that said Penthouse. "I'm a Winchester," he said easily. "I open dividend checks for a living, remember?"

"I thought you wanted to write screenplays." Her tone was faintly accusing. "Or novels. Whatever happened to that?"

"Actually, I started a screenplay," he said.

"But you didn't finish it?"

"Other obligations got in the way. I haven't stopped thinking about it, though. The same way I never stopped thinking about you."

"Smooth line, T." Kelly glanced over at him. "But somehow, I have trouble believing it."

"I guess you don't have to believe it," Jax said. "But it *is* true."

He was leaning casually, nonchalantly against the wall of the elevator, feet crossed in front of him, hands in his pants pockets. His hair was mussed and still wet from the rain. He smiled at her perusal, his eyes warm and very green.

Was this elevator shrinking? Kelly looked up at the numbers that were changing above the door. Eight more floors 'til they reached the penthouse level. What was that old saying, out of the elevator and into the penthouse? *Why* did she ever come up here with him?

"What do you want from me?" she asked, point-blank.

He answered with the same laid-bare honesty. "I want to marry you."

Stunned, Kelly heard a ding as the elevator reached the penthouse floor, and the doors glided open. She stared at T. in shock. He held the doors back with one hand and gestured with the other. "After you," he said calmly, as if he hadn't just told her that he wanted to…marry her.

He wanted to marry her.

The initial shock was starting to wear off, and as Kelly walked down the long hotel corridor, she began to laugh. He said he wanted to marry her. What a hoot.

Unperturbed, Jax used a plastic key card to unlock the door and opened it wide, stepping back to let her go in first.

His hotel suite was enormous. It had a spacious living room tastefully done in the same subdued colors that had decorated the lobby. But the best part of the room was the wall of glass that overlooked downtown Boston. The view was breathtaking.

As Kelly walked toward the windows, she saw a set of French doors that led into a huge bedroom. The bed itself was almost the size of her entire apartment. She pulled her eyes away, not wanting to be caught staring.

T. Jackson hung his wet sport jacket on the back of a chair, and as Kelly turned to look at him, she saw that his shirt was wet. He had been soaked by the rain clear through his jacket.

Slowly, she put her backpack down on the floor.

He smiled at her as he pulled off his tie and kicked

off his shoes. "I'll be right back," he said, unbuttoning his shirt. "Help yourself to the bar."

There was a wet bar on the wall next to the TV, and Kelly tried to focus her attention on the various bottles of alcohol and soda, rather than the glimpse of hard, tan muscles she'd seen before T. had left the room.

She poured herself a tall glass of seltzer, added a few ice cubes and turned to look around.

There were a number of books scattered about the room. Two of them were Jayne Tyler's most recent releases. A third was a galley copy of what Kelly assumed was to be Jayne's next book, entitled *Love's Sweet Captive*. Seven titles that she recognized from the *New York Times* bestseller list, both fiction and nonfiction, sat on an end table. A week's worth of the *Boston Globe* lay in a pile on the floor. *Premiere* magazine and *Writer's Digest* were open and out on the coffee table, along with several news magazines.

"Grab me a cola from the fridge, will ya, Kel?" Jax called out from the bedroom.

She pulled a can of soda free from a six-pack that was in the refrigerator as Jackson appeared in the bedroom door. He was wearing a pair of faded jeans and a smile, turning a T-shirt rightside out.

Kelly tried not to stare. It wasn't as if she hadn't ever seen him without a shirt on before. But, Lord, he looked good. His body was well-toned and his skin was smooth and lightly tanned.

His muscles rippled as he pulled his shirt over his head and down across his broad chest.

"What do you really want from me?" Kelly heard herself ask. Her voice sounded faint and breathless.

His fingers brushed hers as he took the can of soda

from her hand. "I told you," he said easily, his teeth flashing as he shot her a brief smile. "I want to marry you. I wanted to marry you seven years ago, Kelly, and I *still* want to marry you."

Kelly felt a prick of anger and she clung to it, unable to deal with the other emotions that were assailing her. "After all this time, *you're* finally ready—"

"No." He shook his head, his green eyes unyielding, pinning her in place. "*You're* finally ready."

"The hell I am," she said with an exasperated laugh. "I've just gotten out of one foolish marriage. Do you really think I'd be so eager to get into another right now?"

"Do you really think marriage to me would be foolish?" he countered.

"Absolutely."

T. took a step toward her, setting his can of soda on the coffee table. "Why?"

He moved another step forward. His eyes were green crystal, his face unsmiling and serious.

Kelly crossed her arms defensively, determined to stand her ground. "Oh, come on, T.," she said. "Why do you think?"

"I don't know," he said softly, shaking his head. "Seven years ago, you seemed to think marrying me was a good idea."

T. Jackson had that burning light in his eyes as he took yet another step toward her. He was getting too close, close enough to be able to reach out and touch her.

Kelly stepped around him, bending down to pick up her backpack and jacket. "I took you seriously then because I was too young to know better." She put more space between them. "But I know better now."

She had to leave before the horrible memories of the hurt she had felt when he left brought the pain back. But he was standing between her and the door, blocking her way out of the suite.

"I know I disappointed you," Jackson said softly.

Kelly laughed. "Yeah, I'd say I was disappointed," she agreed. "For God's sake, T., you left the country without even saying goodbye to me!" She pushed past him toward the door. "I've got to go—"

Jax caught her arm. "Please, Kel..." He suddenly wished desperately that real life could be as simple as fiction. He wished he could go back and rewrite some of the scenes in his life. But he'd made so many mistakes with Kelly, it was hard to know where to start. He wished at least he'd had a chance to make love to her, to show her how much he loved her. Suddenly he was glad that he had added that love scene between Jared and Carrie to his book. Their one night of love was what bound them together, and it would keep them bound together even as they faced the trials and tribulations he was going to send their way.

But he and Kelly had had no such night. He had never even said the words *I love you* to her.

She pulled her arm away and stared at him, anger and hurt in her eyes. "I loved you so much, T. But it was just a game to you—"

"No!" He raked his hair back out of his face with his fingers. "That's not true—"

"The truth is, you were doing Kevin a favor by taking me to the prom," she said hotly. "But you went kind of overboard, took it a step too far." She reached for the doorknob, pulling the door open. "Well, not this time, Jackson."

But he pushed the door closed with the palm of one

hand, and brought his other hand up against the door on the other side of her, effectively pinning her between his arms. "No," he said very definitely. "I won't let you run away. You've got to give me a chance to explain."

T. was standing so close, Kelly could feel heat radiating from his body. She could smell his sweet scent, a mixture of after-shave, shampoo and his own, individual familiar aroma.

"God, you even smell the same," she said, looking up into the swirling colors of his eyes. *I give up,* she suddenly wanted to say. *Take me to dinner. Take me anywhere. Take me.*

She knew all she had to do was ask. There was no mistaking the desire she could see in his eyes.

He leaned toward her, as somehow she knew he would, and he kissed her, also as she knew he would. What she didn't expect was the total meltdown she experienced as his lips touched hers.

Her bones became liquid, her muscles useless and her arms, the evil betrayers, wrapped themselves around T. Jackson's neck, pulling him even closer to her. She heard him groan as his tongue pushed past her lips, tasting her, possessing her.

Nothing had changed. Seven years had passed, during which time Kelly had been married and divorced, yet all it took was one kiss from this man and all the old feelings came flooding back. As her fingers became tangled in his soft, blond hair, she tried to stop herself, but she couldn't.

He kissed her, harder, pulling her body in more tightly to him, his hands cupping the softness of her derriere, pressing her hips against him.

He lifted his head then, and Kelly stared into the

turbulence of his eyes. "You know what I want," he said, his voice thick, raspy.

There was no mistaking the hardness of his arousal as it pressed against her stomach. Even though he hadn't asked a question, Kelly nodded, unable to speak.

"I wanted to make love to you the morning after the prom, too." He kissed her neck, her throat, running his hands lightly up her body, touching the sides of her breasts.

She closed her eyes, wanting him to touch her, wanting…

"I wanted you so badly," he whispered. "But you were only sixteen. And I—I didn't even care. I was so crazy in love with you, I couldn't see straight. If Kevin hadn't found us, if he hadn't stopped me, I would've done it. I would have made love to you right there on that beach. You were just a kid, and I didn't even have any protection, and I *still* would have done it, and, Kel, that scared the hell out of me." He shook his head, still amazed that he could have felt so out of control. "So I lost it, I totally lost it. Kevin was beating the crap out of me, and I didn't fight back because I knew I deserved it. And those things he said… I didn't deny it because I couldn't speak, I couldn't even *think*. But I didn't take you to that prom as a favor to your brother. After I saw you in that dress, I begged him to let me take you. I promised him I'd take care of you, and instead I nearly took your virginity—"

Kelly pressed her fingers to his lips. "You weren't the only one there that morning," she said steadily. "I was there, too. And I wanted you as much as you wanted me."

"Kel, you were a kid—"

"So what, T.? I knew what I wanted."

"How could you have known?" he asked. "You were only *sixteen*—"

"I'm not sixteen anymore," she said.

And then she kissed him.

It was a kiss of passion and need, filled with fire and heat and the promise that all they'd started seven years ago would not remain unfinished business. Not for long.

Kelly's backpack dropped to the floor as Jackson pushed her jacket off her shoulders. He heard her inhale sharply as his hands caressed her arms, and he was overcome by the need to touch more of her, all of her. He tugged at her shirt, yanking it free from the waistband of her pants, and groaned as his fingers found the soft, warm skin of her back and her belly. He was lost, lost in the depth of her kisses, consumed by wanting her. Even after all those years, his control was still shot to hell when he held her in his arms. He was possessed, utterly, totally possessed by his burning need.

She moved away from him slightly to pull her shirt over her head. As if in a dream, Jax watched his hands unfasten the front clasp of her bra, releasing the soft fullness of her breasts. He wanted to take his time, to look at her, to touch her slowly, but he was on fire, and he couldn't hold back. He touched her almost roughly, driven nearly mad by the heavy weight of her breasts in his palms. Greedily he lowered his head and drew one taut nipple into his mouth, hungrily tugging, sucking until she cried out with pleasure.

Kelly pulled at his shirt then, and he quickly yanked it off. She reached out to touch him lightly, and the sensation was too exquisite, too intense. He crushed her to him, exalting in the feeling of her skin against his as he kissed her frantically. He was unable to think coherently, unable to think at all.

Jax felt her fingers at the waistband of his jeans, unfastening the button, tugging at the zipper.

"Kel," he groaned, knowing that if she touched him there, he'd never be able to turn back. "Kel, what are we doing?"

Her laughter was low and sexy. "Don't you know?"

He kissed her neck, her throat, letting his hands explore her body. Her hair felt like silk, her skin like satin. His fingers swept lower, and he realized with an electric jolt of pleasure that her leggings were gone. She'd somehow kicked off her cowboy boots and her pants, and now stood before him, naked.

She was beautiful—incredibly, perfectly beautiful.

He felt her tugging at his jeans, pushing them down.

"Oh, Jackson," he heard her whisper as she freed him from the confines of his shorts. And then she touched him. He nearly lost it right then and there, simply from the touch of her hand.

Seven years. For seven years he'd been waiting for this moment.

He touched the softness between her legs, feeling the heat and wetness that proclaimed her desire. Kelly opened herself to him, pressing against his exploring fingers. "Please, T.," she breathed, "I need you *now...*"

She had a condom. She must've had it in her backpack. She handed it to him and, as quickly as he could with shaking hands, he covered himself.

And then the waiting was over.

He lifted her up, and with one fierce thrust, he was inside of her. She cried out with pleasure as he plunged into her again and again.

Kelly's back was still to the door, her arms and legs wrapped tightly around T. as she moved with him. She'd never made love like this before. She'd never felt so desperately wanted, so fiercely desired. T.'s eyes were lit with a wild passion that both excited her and frightened her—frightened her because she suddenly doubted that making love to him once would be enough.

He pulled her down with him then, down onto the floor. He covered her body with his own, increasing the tempo of his movements. She met each thrust by lifting her hips, pushing him even more deeply into her. His hands and mouth were everywhere, adding to the sensations, driving her closer and closer to release.

And suddenly she was flying, hurtling through space as waves and waves of pleasure rocketed through her.

"Yes," she heard T. say through the storm that possessed her. "Come on, Kelly." And somehow, some way, she went even higher.

Jax had only imagined how good this would be, but his imagination hadn't even come close to the reality. As the last tremors passed through her, she gazed up at him. "Oh, T., we should have done this seven years ago," she breathed, still moving with him.

She smiled up at him then, and it was the love he was so sure he saw in her eyes that pushed him over the edge.

He exploded. It was amazing, incredible, impossibly wonderful. He wanted to laugh and cry and...

And she held him tightly, her arms around him, until his breathing slowed. He rolled off of her then, pulling her into his arms. He could feel Kelly watching him staring at the ceiling for several long moments before he glanced at her out of the corners of his eyes. He laughed, not without a certain amount of embarrassment.

"I have such amazing finesse," he said, more to himself than her. "I had seven years to plan the perfect way to make love to you for the first time, and what do I do? I don't even take you into the bedroom. I end up nailing you to the wall."

She laughed. "Is that what that's called? I liked it a lot."

Jackson moved his left arm out from underneath her so he could use it to support his head as he looked down into her eyes. "I'm glad," he murmured.

She reached up to push his hair back from his face.

Jax's smile was sheepish and utterly charming. "I really wasn't planning for this to happen, you know, for us to make love. I was totally unprepared. I'm glad you had a condom." He leaned down and kissed her, a long, lazy, unhurried kiss.

Kelly closed her eyes, feeling her heart begin to beat faster. Could she really want him again? Already?

When Jackson swung her up into his arms and carried her through the bedroom into the huge bathroom, she didn't protest. He set her down in the big shower stall and gently washed them both clean, and still she didn't protest. By the time he had wrapped her in the thick, white hotel towel, she was on fire again. And from the looks of things, he was, too.

He pulled her to his bed and sat down, holding her on his lap. He kissed her, another slow, leisurely kiss that made her tremble. As he held her close, she could feel his heart pounding and knew that he hadn't gotten her out of his system any more than she had removed him from hers.

Once had definitely not been enough.

"Kelly, why did you give in?" Jax murmured into her neck as his hands caressed the smooth, clean length of her body. "Don't get me wrong—I love it that you're here, but I'm just...kind of surprised."

She pulled back slightly to look at him. "I guess I figured that it's time to move on with my life," she said. "We've both had this attraction for each other for such a long time, and..." *Neither one of us would ever really have been free until we proved that sex between us wasn't the magnificent event we'd imagined,* she wanted to say, but couldn't. Because in reality, making love to T. Jackson had been far, far more magnificent than any fantasy she'd dreamed. Instead of being freed by finally making love to this man, she had simply made the chains that bound her to him that much tighter.

But Jax couldn't read her mind, and the words he heard filled him with happiness. She was ready to move on with her life, and it sure seemed as if she'd chosen to move in his direction. "Kelly, I want to make love to you again," he whispered. "If that's okay with you."

She told him just how okay it was with a kiss, and he pulled her back with him onto the bed.

Maybe this time, thought Kelly. Maybe making love to him this time would chase his memory back to where it belonged—securely in the past.

Chapter 8

Kelly awoke as dawn was beginning to edge its way past the hotel room curtains. T. lay in the big bed beside her, his arm possessively draped across her, holding her close, her back against his chest.

She felt the familiar jolt of sexual excitement that always shot through her when she was near this man. It flared into full-blown desire as she felt his most masculine part pressing into her leg.

T. Jackson even wanted her in his sleep.

Being desired so intensely gave her a powerfully strong feeling. It was similar to the way she'd felt as a kid when she'd climbed out onto the roof of the house. She felt daring, bold and adventurous. She felt an adrenaline high, a rush.

But that wasn't the kind of feeling she wanted from a relationship.

She wanted to feel safe and warm. She wanted to

feel secure. She wanted to be cherished, not hungered for.

T. looked so peaceful, so serene, so content as he slept. With his hair disheveled, an unruly jumble of waves falling down across his forehead, with his long, dark lashes lying against his smooth, tanned cheeks, he was, truly, the most beautiful man she'd ever seen. He was funny, smart, bright and fun to be around. But he'd broken her heart once, and there was no reason to believe that he wouldn't do it again. No, she could not let herself love him again.

How could you love T. *again,* when you never stopped loving him? a little voice in her head asked.

But she *had* stopped loving him. She could remember the exact time, the exact hour it had happened.

That was when you *wanted* to stop loving him, the voice said. It doesn't mean you really stopped. People can't just turn their feelings off like a light switch. You still love him.

No, Kelly thought almost desperately. She *didn't* love T., and she could prove it.

Quietly she slipped out of bed and went into the living room. She dressed quickly and grabbed her backpack and jacket, and crept out of the room and out of the hotel.

Standing at the underground trolley stop, she waited for the train that would take her home.

See, she told herself, she didn't love him. If she loved him, she wouldn't have been able to walk away.

Okay, the little voice in her head said. So how come you're crying?

Dear Kelly,
Toilet paper.

They found my book and took it away and now they use the pages for toilet paper.

The warden laughs at the look on my face, at the tears I can't keep from my eyes, knowing he has at last found a way to hurt me.

You come to me then, for the first time appearing when others are around. They can't see you. They don't know it is your strength that keeps me from crumbling.

"Don't cry," you order me, your eyes fiery with determination. "Keep your head up. You've got that book practically memorized anyway. So what if they take the paper that it's written on? They can't take your memory. It's in your head, T., you can write it again."

You look so beautiful, trembling with your conviction. I smile at you, and I am rewarded by your bright grin.

The warden frowns and sends me back to my cell.

I love you.

Love, T.

Jax woke up with a smile on his face that faded as soon as he rolled over and saw that he was alone in his bed.

"Kel?" he called out, going first into the bathroom and then out in the living room.

He saw right away that her things were gone. He looked around for a note, thinking maybe she had an appointment and she didn't want to wake him.

But there was no note.

Why would she leave like that, without saying goodbye? Why would she slip out of his room as if last night had been nothing more than a casual one-night stand?

Fear hit him, squeezing all of the air out of his lungs.

No.

No, he wouldn't believe that. Things had gotten pretty intense last night. She must've gotten scared and felt the need for some time alone, to think about what was going on, about what was happening between them.

He crossed the room and picked up the telephone, quickly punching in her number.

She answered on the second ring. "Hello?"

Jackson took a deep breath, determined not to let his paranoia show. "Hey," he said, his voice light. "Good morning."

"Jackson," she said.

Not a very enthusiastic greeting. And was that trepidation he heard in her voice? Or were his insecurities making him imagine things?

"I missed you this morning." He still kept his voice easygoing. "I'm dying to see you again. What do you say I pick you up in about an hour and we have lunch?"

There was a brief moment of silence, during which time Jackson died over and over and over again. *Say yes,* he prayed. *Please say yes.*

"I'd planned to write all day," Kelly finally answered. "I'm not as far along as I'd hoped to be with this story and..."

It sounded like a lame excuse. But Jax understood what it meant to need time to write, so maybe it really wasn't. "How about I pick you up at six? You should be ready for a break by then. We can have dinner."

"I don't think so."

Her words echoed in the great, big, heavy silence that followed. Jax slowly sat down. His heart was in his throat as he finally said, "Kelly, what's going on? I don't—I don't understand."

"T., I already told you that I don't want to become involved with you," she said softly. "I'm not ready to be in a relationship right now."

All that was left of last night's happiness crashed and burned. Jax's knuckles were white as he clutched the telephone. But still he managed to keep his voice calm. "I think you're too late, Kel. I don't know what you'd call last night, but I'd say at this point we've started something that's pretty involved."

"Last night we were finishing something, Jackson," Kelly said quietly. "Not starting it."

"Kelly, please don't say that." Desperation was starting to creep into his voice.

"I'm sorry. I've got to go—"

"Wait, please! Talk to me—"

But she'd already hung up.

Kelly sat in front of her computer, trying to find the right words to finish her latest manuscript's final love scene. This was the hardest part of writing romances. At least it was for her. She kept her thesaurus handy, and had even made a list of words such as *tempestuous* and *untamed* but when she reread the scenes, there always seemed to be something missing.

The telephone rang again and she closed her eyes, trying not to listen as her answering machine intercepted yet another of T. Jackson's telephone calls.

"Kelly, I know you're home." His normally easygoing voice sounded tight, his words clipped. "So answer the damn phone. If you don't, I'm coming over."

She swore softly under her breath, then shut down the power to her computer.

The spring day had dawned warm and sunny after yesterday's dismal rain. It was a perfect day to go running. And now seemed like an especially perfect time.

She changed quickly into a pair of running shorts and her sneakers, pulling a T-shirt on over an athletic bra. Automatically she reached up to pull her hair back into a ponytail, then smiled as she realized that with her new short hairstyle, that was no longer possible. She tied her house key onto her shoelace, trying not to think about T. Jackson.

She'd spent the entire day trying not to think about him. She hadn't thought once about the way his green eyes seemed to glow as he made love to her. She hadn't thought about his rich laugh or the sexy catch that she heard in his voice when he wanted her. And she certainly hadn't thought once about his hard, lean, muscular body, or about that golden tan that intriguingly covered every inch of him.

No, she hadn't thought about him once. She'd thought about him too many times to count.

But she was more than a walking hormone. And there was more to life than good sex.

She wanted a man who would stick around for the rest of his life, not just for a few years until he got tired of her.

But what would it hurt, that pesky little voice popped into her head and said, if you spent the summer with T.? Spend one last summer with a man who drives you wild, *then* start dating only safe, down-to-earth types.

No, she couldn't do that. The emotional risk was too great.

What emotional risk? the voice argued. You say you don't still love the guy. You say you're not going to fall in love with him again, no way—

Damn right. And the best way to not fall in love with T. was to avoid him. There was no doubt about that.

She closed her apartment door, checking to see that it was locked, then quickly went down the stairs. She pushed open the screen door at a run, went out on the porch, down the steps—

And skidded to a stop to keep from slamming into T.

How the hell did he get over here so quickly? Cell phone, she realized instantly. Of course. He must've called her on his cell phone. So much for making an easy escape. So much for avoiding him.

His face looked hard. There was definitely a determined set to his jaw, but his eyes held more than a glimmer of hurt as he stared at her.

"Going somewhere?" he asked.

Kelly sighed. "Yeah, I was going to go running."

"Running away, you mean," he said tightly.

"You're really angry at me." Her heart sank further. She had hoped he'd see that this was for the best.

He laughed, a quick burst of exasperated air. "Did you actually think I wouldn't be angry? Or hurt?" He shook his head. "God, Kelly, what are you trying to prove?"

"T., I didn't mean to hurt you." Her eyes filled with

tears and she fought to blink them back. "I thought…"

"What?" T. pulled her chin up so that Kelly was forced to look him in the eye. "What did you think? That I wouldn't care? That I'd just walk away, disappear, stop bothering you? Say, 'thanks, it was a lot of fun?'"

"Yes," she said honestly, then backed away from the sudden flare of anger in his stormy eyes. "I thought that if we made—if we *had* sex, we'd both realize that the attraction between us wasn't real, that it was based on fantasy, on the past."

He turned away from her, screwing his eyes shut as if in sudden pain. "*That's* what you meant when you said you wanted to move ahead with your life. I thought you were talking about having a future with me, but damn it, you were exorcising me, weren't you?"

When she didn't answer, he turned back to face her. "Weren't you?"

Kelly stared into his accusing eyes, and felt a tear escape and roll down her cheek. "Yes," she whispered.

"Well, did it work?" T.'s voice was raspy. "Did you get me out of your system, Kel? 'Cause it sure as hell didn't work for me."

"I don't know," Kelly said, another tear joining the first.

Jax stared at her. Her eyes were so big in her pale face. She looked little more than a child. But she was no child. Not anymore. They'd both proved that last night.

"Did you really think that all I wanted was to make love to you?" He felt tears burning his own eyelids.

"No, not make love, you called it sex. Is that really all it was to you, Kelly? Sex? Just a one-goddamned-night stand? God, I made *love* to you last night."

His voice shook with emotion, and he turned away, wiping the tears from his eyes. "Goddamn it, Kelly," he whispered. "*Goddamn* you."

"I'm sorry," she said.

"Are you?" He turned back to her. "Then have dinner with me. Spend time with me. Let this thing between us have a chance—"

"No." She realized how brusque she sounded, and tried to soften it. "T., I can't, I—"

"Come to the Cape with me." He took a step toward her, reached for her. "Please, Kelly. God, I'm begging you—"

She moved away. "No!"

He shook his head, defeated, and turned away, heading for his car. But he'd only gone a few steps before he came back. As Kelly watched, he took a business card out of his wallet and held it out to her.

"Take it," he ordered her, and Kelly reluctantly reached for it. "It's my phone number on Cape Cod. In case you need me for anything. In case…" His voice shook again, and he took a deep breath. "This is not over," he said, gazing directly into her eyes. "I'm under your skin—you just don't know it yet. But I'm under there and you're not going to be able to forget me. Especially now, after last night. If that really was just sex for you, Kelly, imagine how good making love to me could be."

Kelly stood staring, long after his car had disappeared.

Chapter 9

Dear Kelly,

For the first time in months I have hope.

A piece of paper has appeared, slipped by unknown hands through the crack under the heavy wooden door to my cell. It lies on the damp dirt floor, white and shining in the dim morning light.

I pick it up slowly, carefully.

It is a card. The paper is a thick linen blend and I run my fingers lightly over the texture of the fibers. It has the feel of a wedding invitation.

I turn it over. There's a picture on the front. A drawing.

A white dove flies up to the sky, escaping the bars of a prison cell. Inside the darkness of the cell, a single candle burns. It is wrapped in barbed wire.

My hands tremble as I open the card. There is writing inside—plain block letters. In English.

"Jackson Winchester, we know you are there," I read. "We are working and praying for your immediate and unconditional release."

There is no signature, but I know who it is from.

Amnesty International.

One month later I am free.

"**O**h, please, don't tell me *that's* your breakfast." Stefanie looked with pointed distaste at the cold slice of pizza Jax held in one hand as he opened the refrigerator with the other.

"All right, I won't tell you," he said, pulling out a bottle of beer and opening it.

"When was the last time you shaved?" She followed him up the stairs and into his office.

The spacious room had big windows that looked out over the bay, and an entire wall of bookshelves filled with books of all shapes and sizes, covering a vast plethora of subjects. Jax's computer was set up so that he could look out over the water with a simple turn of his head, but directly above the monitor was a huge corkboard to which he'd pinned information on his current characters and a brief list of the major plot points of his story.

There was a large oak table in the room, with several comfortable chairs placed around it. A couch ran along another wall. The floors were hardwood and the ceiling was high, angling up dramatically.

Jax stood in front of the windows, eating the cold pizza and staring at the sunlight on the water. There was a boat way out, almost beyond the edge of the horizon, and he could see only the tiny speck of its red sail against the brilliant blue sky.

He scratched the back of the hand that held the bottle of beer with the rough stubble on his chin. When *had* he last shaved? But who cared, really? "Why? Are guests coming today?"

"Just Emilio," Stefanie said.

Jax turned to look at her, smiling grimly after he took a long swig of beer. "Thank God. For a minute I thought we were going to get a royal visit from the King or Queen of Winchester."

Stefanie laughed. "Someday you're going to have children of your own, and you better hope they treat *you* with a little more respect than you treat our parents."

His eyes clouded, and he looked back out the window. "I'm never going to have children."

"Ooh, ready to do some wallowing, are we? Poor baby—"

"Don't start," Jackson said sharply.

There was a long silence. The red sail had disappeared down behind the curve of the earth. What would it be like to be on that little boat right now? Out of sight of the land, nothing but the ocean and the sky...

"When was the last time you slept?"

Jax shrugged. "Probably shortly before the last time I shaved."

"Was that two days ago?" she asked. "Or three?"

He turned to look at her. His sister was a picture of health, dressed in her shiny Lycra workout clothes. Her sneakers were so new that Jax almost had to shield his eyes from the glare. Her hair was pulled back off her elegant face, and she wore a light coat of makeup. She was on her way to the fitness club.

"Who knows?" he answered. "I'm in the midst of

a creative spurt. I'm not keeping track of pedestrian things like sleeping and eating.''

"A creative spurt." She crossed her arms skeptically. ''How many pages have you written?''

"Creativity and output aren't necessarily connected,'' he said, somewhat loftily.

"That many?''

He was silent, staring once again out the window.

"You still want me to screen your calls?''

"Yeah," he said. ''I don't want to talk to anyone, except…''

"Kelly," she finished for him.

He didn't bother to say anything. Kelly wasn't going to call. He'd waited for two weeks, and he knew with a certainty that, as each day passed, it was less and less likely she would.

"Jax, maybe it's time to move on," Stefanie said quietly. ''If you're going to give up, then do it. Give up. But don't sit here feeling sorry for yourself—''

"If I wanted therapy, I would've called my shrink.'' He saw a flash of hurt in her eyes, and he felt like a jerk. ''I'm sorry.''

Stef used the toe of her brilliant new sneaker to rub at an imaginary spot in the carpet. Dressed as she was, with her perfectly coiffed hair and her flawlessly applied makeup, it didn't seem possible that she was the one who'd refused to believe he was dead. She was the one who'd marched into that hellhole of a Central American country with the help of Amnesty International's London office and demanded to see either Jax's remains or the location where he was being held.

Stefanie, who had always seemed more concerned with getting her nails done and shopping at Saks, had almost single-handedly set up the letter-writing campaign that had secured his release.

He owed her his freedom, maybe even his life. Definitely his life.

"The publisher called again about that book you started," Stefanie said. "You know, the collection of letters? They're waiting for the final few chapters. Why don't you send it, Jax? I know you've finished it."

"I'm waiting to find out if that book's going to have a happy ending."

She shook her head. "How long do you intend to wait?"

"I don't want to talk about it."

"If you don't want to talk to me," Stef said, "maybe you *should* think about calling that psychologist...what was his name? Dr. Burnham."

Jax stood silently, just watching her.

"Call him," she urged. "Or call Kelly. Do *something*, darling. I'll see you later."

His sister turned and left the room, closing the door softly behind her.

With a sigh, Jax turned back to his computer.

His main characters had run into each other downtown on the Boston Common. They had exchanged pleasantries. It was all so polite and proper, yet they both couldn't help but think about the night they'd made love.

With breathtaking clarity, Jax had a sudden memory of Kelly lying naked on his hotel room bed, smiling up at him, her blue eyes half closed.

"God *damn* it..." Waves of anger and self-pity flooded him until he felt as if he might drown.

"Why the hell are *you* feeling sorry for yourself?"

Jared's mocking voice cut through Jax's misery. "*I'm* the one who's in a real bitch of a situation. I'm starting to really wonder what you've got in mind here. Carrie's obviously mad as hell at me, and I don't have a clue why. I mean, for crying out loud, *she's* the one who married some other dude."

"Don't use words like *bitch* and *dude*," Jax reminded him tiredly. "You live in the 1860's, or have you forgotten?"

"Look at you." Jared ignored Jax's question. "You look like total crap—"

"*Crap.* Another fine word for a historical romance hero."

"—you haven't showered or shaved in days, and you're drinking beer at nine o'clock in the morning—"

"Morning, night, what's the difference anyway?" muttered Jax. "One's got the sun, the other doesn't. Big deal."

"So that's it then?" Jared asked, one eyebrow raised in surprise. "You're giving up on Kelly, just like that?"

Jax didn't answer right away. He just turned to stare out the window as he drank the last few drops of his beer. "I don't know what else to do," he finally said.

"Well, okay, but giving up is really stupid," Jared said. "You automatically lose when you give up. Think about all the heroes in your books. Think about Hank in *Night of the Raven*. He didn't give up when Anna told him she'd fill his hide with buckshot if he as much as set one foot on her ranch. And how about Daniel in *Too Late To Run?* Maggie swore on a stack of Bibles that she'd never fall in love with him, but he won her in the end. Think of all the books you've written—how many *have* you written anyway?"

"One too many, apparently," Jax said dryly.

"Kelly's not going to call," Jared told him.

"Thanks a lot. Rub it in, why don't you?"

"You've got to call her."

Jax looked down at the silent telephone that was sitting within arm's reach of his computer. If he called Kelly, she'd refuse to see him. He knew her well enough to know that. No, he was going to have to make her an offer that she couldn't refuse.

And in a sudden flash of inspiration, he knew just what to offer her. "No." He smiled. "*I'm* not going to call her."

The telephone was ringing as Kelly unlocked the door to her apartment. She was still breathing hard from her three-mile run. Her skin was slick with perspiration, and her clothes were soaked. But she unlocked the door quickly and bolted for the phone. Maybe it was T.

But you don't *want* him to call, she scolded herself as she picked up the kitchen phone. "Hello?" she said breathlessly.

"May I speak to Kelly O'Brien please?" an unfamiliar female voice asked.

Disappointment. She tried to ignore it as she opened the refrigerator door and pulled out a bottle of seltzer.

"Yeah, this is Kelly." The seltzer exploded slightly as she twisted off the cap, spraying her with cool water. She took a large swallow of the bubbling soda right from the bottle.

"Kelly, this is Stefanie Winchester. I don't know if you remember me. We met at that university lecture a few weeks ago?"

T. Jackson's sister. "Of course I remember you.

How are you?'' Kelly asked. *How is T.?* she wanted to ask. *And why hasn't he called me?*

Because you told him not to, she answered her own question.

''Fine, thanks,'' Stefanie said. ''I'm actually calling to ask you for a favor. I'm doing some research for, um, a book, and I need some information on how small-press newspapers are made—everything from planning to layout to printing, and I thought I remembered that Jax had told me you work at the university newspaper…?''

''Yes, that's right.''

''I'm going to be in town tomorrow,'' Stefanie said. ''Would you mind joining me for lunch?''

Lunch. With Jayne Tyler. It smelled very fishy, kind of like *bait.* Now, why did that make her so happy? But if it *was* some kind of lure, she wanted to know about it.

''Lunch isn't necessary,'' Kelly said, testing her theory. ''We can talk right now, on the phone.''

''Well, uh…'' Stefanie hesitated. ''Now's not a really convenient time for me, and I, uh, really would like to get together with you, and, well… How about twelve-thirty at the Bookseller Café?''

''Stefanie, did Jackson put you up to this?'' Kelly asked with her usual bluntness. She took another long drink of seltzer.

Stefanie laughed. ''Yes,'' she admitted. ''He did. He told me if you refused to come to lunch, I should offer to read your latest manuscript, you know, as a bribe.''

Now Kelly laughed, pressing the cold bottle against her forehead. She watched as droplets of sweat dripped onto the tiled floor. ''He's shameless.''

"May I be candid?"

"Of course."

"I don't know what happened between you two," Stefanie said, "but he's been an absolute mess ever since he came back from Boston."

Kelly felt a flash of pain as she remembered the hurt she'd last seen in T.'s eyes. She really hadn't meant to hurt him. She'd been carrying around guilt and remorse for two weeks now, wishing she'd somehow handled the entire affair differently.

She thought about T. Jackson all the time, because of the guilt. Every time she saw a tall, blond man, her heart leapt into overdrive, no doubt because she wanted another chance to apologize to T.

If she could turn back time, she would probably agree to go to Cape Cod with him for the summer. Not because she particularly wanted to go, she reassured herself, although as the mercury climbed higher and higher in the thermometer, it was difficult *not* to think about the cool, blue ocean and the fresh breezes sweeping across the beaches. Never mind how often she thought about a certain pair of eyes that changed color like the sea.

The truth was, she didn't want to feel responsible for that wounded look T. had had on his face the morning after they'd made love. She'd seen that same look in her own mirror the first few months after he'd left for London without telling her. The look was there again when he didn't show up for her eighteenth birthday.

"Will you come?" Stefanie asked.

"My manuscripts aren't perfect," Kelly said. "In fact, I'm having a real tough time finishing my second one. And I can't figure out what's wrong with the first one.''

"Jayne Tyler to the rescue, darling," Stefanie said. "If anyone can help you, it is she. Can I expect to see you tomorrow?"

"Yes," Kelly said decidedly. "Will Jackson be there?"

"Do you want him there?"

Kelly was silent, finishing off the last of the seltzer. "Yeah," she finally said. "I guess I do." That way she'd get her chance to apologize again.

"I'm not sure what his schedule's like," Stefanie said breezily. "I've got to run. Bring whichever manuscript you want. See you tomorrow, Kelly."

Kelly hung up the phone and headed for the shower, feeling lighter than she had in weeks.

Jax settled himself in the beach chair next to Stefanie as she opened one eye and glanced over at him. She took in his freshly shaved face and clean hair, and, most obviously, his smile.

"Well, well, if the smelly little frog hasn't turned back into the handsome prince," she murmured, closing her eyes and turning her face to a better angle to catch the sun.

"What do you think I should wear tomorrow?" Jax asked, pulling off his T-shirt and dropping the chair back into a full reclining position.

"Since when do you ask me for fashion advice, darling?" Stefanie opened both eyes to look at him this time.

"If I were writing this," Jax mused, "I'd have the hero show up in an impeccably tailored suit, looking like a million bucks, never mind that the weatherman's predicting another hundred-degree day for tomorrow.''

''Fictional characters are so nice,'' Stefanie said with a sigh, ''because they never sweat unless you want them to.''

The sun felt warm on Jax's face, and a wave of fatigue hit him. ''If I fall asleep, wake me up in a couple of hours. I don't want to fry.''

''A bathing suit,'' Stefanie said. ''You should wear a bathing suit and one of those disgustingly sexy undershirt things that reveal more than they cover. As long as it's going to be hotter than hell, you might as well look good while you sweat. Have you ever noticed that when an athlete sweats, it's sexy? But a soggy businessman, now, that's an entirely different story.''

Stefanie's watch alarm went off and she put on her hat, careful now to keep her face out of the sun. She only exposed her face to the sun for ten minutes each day. While crow's-feet looked good on men when they aged, women had to be careful.

She glanced back at her brother, but he was already fast asleep.

Dear Kelly,
I am writing this on a real piece of paper with a real pen as I sit on this 727 heading north to Miami.

I am free.

I am flying first-class, and the stewardess offers me champagne, but Stefanie, my sister, shakes her head no. She seems to think I've picked up some nasty bugs during my stay in the tropical wilds of Central America. Her doctors have advised her to let me eat or drink nothing besides bottled water and fresh vegetables until they have checked me out.

There's a hospital bed and a bevy of doctors waiting for me at Mass. General Hospital. Stef tells me she's arranged for a private room, and I laugh. She doesn't get the joke, and I explain— I've spent the last twenty months in solitary. I don't want a private room.

I'll be in the hospital for three or four weeks undergoing medical tests. They'll also be fattening me up. I guess I'm a little malnourished right now.

The warden let me shower and gave me clean clothes before I was released. I have lost so much weight and my beard and hair are so long, I didn't recognize myself in the mirror.

I want to see you, but I don't want you to see me like this. So I'll wait until I'm out of the hospital to call you.

Tonight I will sleep on a bed with real sheets, but I will still dream about you.

I love you.

Love, T.

When Kelly walked into the café, Stefanie was already there, sitting on the outside porch, waiting for her. The older woman waved from the table where she was sitting.

She was alone. No T. Jackson.

Kelly was surprised. What was the point of using Jayne Tyler for bait if T. wasn't even going to bother to show up? Unless he had something else in mind...

The two women greeted each other as Kelly started

to sit down across from Stefanie, placing her briefcase on the floor.

"Oh, sit over here." Stef patted the chair next to hers. "It's so nice to be able to look out on the street."

With a shrug and a smile, Kelly changed seats.

"Did you bring your manuscript?" Stefanie asked.

"Are you kidding?" Kelly was amused. "No one in their right mind would pass up an opportunity to get a critique from Jayne Tyler."

"Let me have it now, so I don't forget to get it from you."

Kelly pulled the heavy manila envelope out of her briefcase and handed it to Stefanie, who set it on the table next to her.

She sat still, returning Stefanie's gaze steadily as the older woman looked at her closely. She was pale, she knew, because she hadn't had much of a chance to get out in the sun. She still ran, but in the very early mornings, just as the sun was starting to rise. The rest of the day she spent inside, in the infernal heat of her apartment, slaving at her computer.

As Stefanie looked at her, Kelly fought the urge to put on her sunglasses, to cover up the dark smudges she knew were under her eyes, the shadows that betrayed the fact that she hadn't been sleeping well for quite some time.

But Stefanie didn't comment. She just smiled and picked up her menu. "What do you say we order before we talk? I'm starving."

"But..." It came out involuntarily.

Stefanie looked at her, eyebrows delicately raised, waiting for her to continue.

What the hell, Kelly thought, and asked, "Isn't Jackson going to join us?" She only wanted a chance to apologize, to clear the air between them.

"He wasn't sure when he could get over here," Stefanie glanced down at her menu, "if at all. I hear the crab salad is wonderful."

Bemused, Kelly opened her menu. If T. Jackson was playing some kind of game with her, he just won a point. She was confused. If he was going to go to all this trouble to get her together with his sister, it seemed kind of silly for him not to show up.

After the waiter came up to their table and took their order, they began to talk. Stefanie was easygoing and self-confident, like her brother, and socially quite adept. She gracefully steered their conversation from one light topic to another. Although the two women came from entirely different backgrounds, they had a lot in common.

Before Kelly knew it, their lunches had arrived.

Stefanie somehow managed to eat and converse at the same time, and without ever talking with her mouth full.

"So I went into the fitness center—" the elegant blonde took a sip of her water "—expecting my personal trainer to be some kind of Nazi drill sergeant, or, even worse, a muscle-bound Amazon commando bitch, and Lord help me, but I must have done *some*-thing worthwhile at *some* time in my life. I look up into *the* most soulful pair of brown eyes that I've ever seen in my life. And those eyes just happened to be attached to this incredible Roman god of a man. His name was Emilio Dicarrio, he told me in this wonderful Italian accent.'' She gestured at Kelly with her fork. ''I'm telling you, it was love at first sight, for both of us.'' Another sip of water. ''At first I thought, God, how tacky. Falling in love with your personal trainer—that's almost as gauche as having a thing for your shrink. Then I thought, he's a gold digger, just after my money. That's what Jax thought, too. But Emilio is one of the few people that I've ever met who's totally happy with his life. He's living in the United States, working in a job he likes. I tell you, the man's *content*. I offered him a chance to do some modeling for some of Jayne's book covers. He did a few photo shoots, but then turned down all the other offers because he thought the work was dull.''

''He sounds perfect,'' Kelly said. ''What's the catch?''

The blond woman's gray eyes were suddenly subdued. ''He wants me to marry him.''

''That's a problem?'' Kelly asked.

''Emilio is only twenty-two years old. He's a baby. He's ten years younger than I am.''

''So?''

''So when he's forty, I'll be fifty.'' She shuddered. ''Darling, it's too terrible to consider.''

''But that's eighteen years away,'' Kelly protested.

Stefanie shrugged, taking a sip of her iced tea. ''So tell me.'' Her gray eyes were suddenly sharp and slightly accusing. ''Why did you come to lunch today? Was it purely mercenary, only to drop off your manuscript, or were you hoping to see my brother?''

Kelly returned her gaze steadily. ''I wanted to apologize to Jackson. I'm afraid I treated him badly.''

"You know, when he came back from Central America—" Stefanie stopped, looking at the puzzled expression on Kelly's face. "Don't tell me. He never told you what happened in Central America?"

"Was that before or after he went to London?"

"Oh, God." Stefanie sat back in her chair, staring sightlessly down at her plate. Why hadn't Jax told Kelly? He had a nearly completed 250-page manuscript of letters to her. Letters that he'd obviously never even told her about...

"Why? What happened in Central America?" Kelly asked curiously.

"No." Stefanie looked up at her again. "Jax will tell you if he wants you to know."

The waiter approached the table. "Ms. Winchester," he murmured. "Phone call."

Stefanie stood. "Excuse me. Maybe that's Jax."

Kelly put her chin in her hand and watched the traffic, both in the street and on the sidewalk. The café looked out on quirky Newbury Street in downtown Boston, so there was a wide variety of people passing by. Overheated men in business suits, delivery men without their shirts on, modern hippies in long, flowing skirts, teenagers with more earrings and nose rings than Kelly could count, tourists in Bermuda shorts and T-shirts with cameras around their perspiring necks....

From out of this teeming mass of humanity, Kelly suddenly saw him. T. Jackson Winchester the Second. His golden hair reflected the sunshine. His eyes were covered by his sunglasses, but the rest of his face looked calm and relaxed. He was wearing...

Kelly swallowed. He was wearing a colorful bathing

suit and a tank top that was nearly nonexistent. The only thing missing was his surfboard.

As he walked down the street, his muscles rippled. As Kelly watched, he turned in to the entrance of the café and opened the door. He hadn't spotted her yet, but it wouldn't be long.

She took a cooling sip of her water, and then there he was. Standing in front of her.

"Hey," he said with a quick smile. "Mind if I sit down?"

Silently she shook her head, trying not to stare at him.

Up close, she could see the light sheen of sweat on his muscles. His shirt was white, matching his teeth, contrasting with his tanned skin. A sudden vivid picture of T. Jackson wearing nothing at all popped into her mind.

She took another sip of water, wishing she could be hosed down. It was much too hot today.

T. sat down across from her, but he kept his sunglasses on. It was unnerving not to be able to see his eyes.

"How are you?" He leaned forward and casually rested his elbows on the table. "How's the writing coming?"

She had missed him.

She hadn't realized it until just now, but somehow she'd let herself get used to him hanging around, following her everywhere. And then when he was gone, something had been missing.

She'd missed his *friendship,* she told herself firmly. Because, face it, that was what their relationship had always been based on. Out of all those years of being close, they had only spent one day as lovers. Well, two, counting the night she'd spent in his hotel room.

Kelly leaned forward, too. "T., I'm really sorry about the way I treated you," she told him. "I don't want you to think that I slept with you as some kind of revenge thing or something like that, because I didn't. I honestly thought it would do us *both* good if we could be free from the past. I didn't mean to hurt you, and I'm sorry if I did."

His smile had faded, but she still couldn't see behind his sunglasses. "Kel, you're apologizing for the best night of my life," he said softly. "Don't do that."

He looked up suddenly, and Kelly turned to see Stefanie returning to their table.

"Well, well, look what the cat dragged in." Stef smiled, stopping to drop a kiss on the top of her brother's head. She turned to Kelly as she sat down. "Sorry about that. The publisher needs some revisions by yesterday. I'm afraid Jayne hasn't been on the ball lately."

"That's the second time you've done that," Kelly said. "You referred to Jayne in the third person, like she's somebody else."

"It's a funny thing about pseudonyms," Jax said easily. "They seem to take on a life of their own." He glanced at his watch. "If you're ready, Stef, I'll get the car and pull it around front." He stood, looking down at Kelly from behind his shades. "Nice seeing you."

He picked Kelly's manuscript up off the table, and left.

She turned to Stefanie, who was signaling the waiter for the check. ''But we didn't talk about small-press newspapers.''

Stefanie smiled. ''Darling, we didn't need to in the first place.''

''But...'' Kelly laughed. ''What just happened here? Did I miss something? Jackson set up this elaborate plan for me to have lunch with you simply to show up, say three sentences and leave? I don't get it.''

Stefanie just smiled.

Chapter 10

Outside the windows of the office, the beach was dark. Jax sat leaning back, his feet up on the conference table, as he read the last few pages of Kelly's manuscript.

It was good. It wasn't perfect, but it was pretty damn good. The heroine was a tough, feisty Katharine Hepburn type. In fact, the whole story read like a 1940s romantic comedy, with crackling, fast-paced dialogue.

In his opinion, the story had two major weaknesses. One was that the hero's motivation seemed unclear and some of his actions were contrived. The second weakness was in the love scenes.

Kelly wasn't comfortable writing those scenes, and it showed. Instead of being sensual explosions of emotion and feelings, they were sketchy and vague. And over much too soon.

Jax glanced at his watch. It was nearly midnight. Too late to call Kelly tonight.

With a sigh, he stood, stretching his muscles, heading toward the kitchen and the cold beer in the refrigerator.

Damn, but Kelly had looked good today. He was glad that he had been wearing his sunglasses, glad that she hadn't seen his eyes. If she had, she would've seen how badly he had missed her, and how much he wanted to be with her. She would have seen how badly he still wanted her.

He opened his beer with a swoosh and took a long sip.

It had nearly killed him to get up from that table after only sitting there with her for a few minutes. But his goal wasn't to have lunch with her. He was aiming for bigger things.

Such as forever.

He'd noticed her trying not to look at his body today. She hadn't been able to hide the flashes of desire that he'd seen in her eyes. Despite what she'd said about getting him out of her system, he knew that the magnetic pull of attraction he felt whenever he was near her was stronger than ever. And he knew she felt it, too.

She said he belonged only in her past, but she was wrong. He knew that he was her future. And she was his.

He would do whatever it took to prove that to her.

Well, almost anything.

He winced, remembering the way Stefanie had damn near chewed his head off in the car this afternoon. She didn't understand why he hadn't told Kelly about Central America.

When exactly was he supposed to have told her?

At Kevin's wedding maybe? Right after she'd dropped her own nuptial bomb?

He'd tried calling her when she was living in California, but Brad had answered the phone. Kelly's husband had told Jax in no uncertain terms that he didn't want him calling his wife. With a husband as jealous as Brad obviously was, there was no way Jax could resume his role in Kelly's life as friend of the family. He wasn't even sure he wanted to resume that role anyway. Instead, he'd stayed away from her for all those years.

So how could he have told her about Central America?

Maybe he was supposed to have told her in between her classes in Boston, as he chased her down the sidewalk. Yeah, he'd had *tons* of time then.

The night that they had made love, he had thought there would be plenty of opportunities to talk to her in the future, to tell her what had happened, what he had been through. But he'd been wrong.

And Jackson didn't want to tell her now. He didn't want her to pity him. He wanted her to love him.

Kelly couldn't sleep.

It was much too hot in her apartment, even with all of the windows open wide and the fans blowing directly at her.

Without the shades pulled down, light from the street lamp on the corner made bright patterns on the walls as it shone through the trees. She stared at them for a while, unwilling to shut her eyes.

Because when she shut her eyes, she saw T. Jackson.

T. Jackson. Looking better than a man had a right to.

T. Jackson. Giving in to his desire, unable even to walk the short distance to the hotel bedroom before he made love to her.

T. Jackson. Dancing with her all those years ago at her junior prom, smiling down into her eyes.

With sudden clarity, Kelly could see T., dressed again in a tuxedo, standing in the church where Kevin had married Beth.

Kelly was one of the bridesmaids. She and Brad flew down to Beth's hometown of Atlanta to take part in the ceremony....

As the organist had begun to play the wedding march, she had followed the other bridesmaids down the aisle. The crowd in the church had all risen to their feet to watch. Kelly had smiled back into the sea of friendly, happy faces until suddenly she'd seen him.

T. Jackson Winchester the Second.

Kevin hadn't mentioned that T. was coming to the wedding.

But he was standing on the groom's side of the church, at the end of the pew closest to the center aisle. His blond hair was cut short, and his face looked pale and gaunt, as if he'd recently been very ill. But he was smiling at her, his eyes warm and so very green.

As she stared at him in shock, his lips moved as he silently spoke her name.

The ceremony passed in a blur, with Kelly standing up and sitting down with Beth's sisters, who were beside her at the front of the church.

Her mind was a whirlwind of thoughts. She'd never expected to see T. again. His estrangement with Kevin had seemed so permanent, so unmendable. The last time she asked Kevin about him, her brother had been vague, saying he thought Jax was still in London, but he wasn't sure.

Yet here he was. In Atlanta, of all places, for Kevin's wedding.

Kelly felt T.'s gaze on her throughout the entire ceremony. When she looked up to meet his eyes, he smiled at her. God, his smile could still take her breath away.

Her gaze flickered nervously toward Brad, who was sitting on the other side of the church. He hadn't wanted to come to this wedding. He hated flying, and he was already worrying about tomorrow morning's flight home. He was staring sightlessly down at the ground, the muscles in his jaw working.

As if he felt her eyes on him, Brad looked up at Kelly. But he didn't smile. He looked at her closely, the way he did a lot lately, as if he weren't sure exactly who she was. As if he couldn't figure out how he'd suddenly wound up married to her.

The events leading up to their marriage *had* happened fast. Kelly would be the first to admit it. She'd met Brad her senior year of high school, during an orientation session at Boston University. He was an upperclassman, and he had, as he later told her, fallen in love with her instantly.

He was tall, like T., and blond, like T., with the same zest for life evident in his winning smile. He was a senior when she was a college freshman, and almost before she knew it, he had taken her virginity and, she thought, her heart.

Carried along on the waves of romance, Kelly had married him in the fall of her sophomore year of college. Four months had passed since then, and now, looking into Brad's shuttered, expressionless blue eyes, she was starting to wonder just what they'd gotten themselves into.

The ceremony finally ended, and then the wedding party posed for pictures. When that was over, Kelly was whisked into a waiting limo with the other bridesmaids. As the big, white car pulled away from the church, she could see T. Jackson standing there, watching her. He lifted his hand in a wave.

It wasn't until the reception that T. caught up with her. Kelly and Brad were standing near the bar, talking to Beth's older sister as the band played an old, slow song. Couples were on the dance floor, swaying to the music.

Kelly spotted T. on the other side of the room, and knew that he was heading in her direction. She felt the urge to run or hide or—

"Kelly."

She looked up into the swirling colors of T. Jackson's eyes. He looked so thin as to be unhealthy, but his eyes were still the same marvelous mix of colors. Had it really been three years since she'd seen him last? Three long years since the night of her junior prom...

"You look beautiful," he said.

His lips curved into a small smile, and as he stepped even closer to her, he reached out and his warm fingers touched her arm, sliding gently down to her hand. As he pulled her toward him, his gaze dropped to her mouth.

He was going to kiss her, right there, right in front of *Brad*—

And he did.

T. Jackson gently brushed her lips with his.

"I need to talk to you." He smiled down at her. "Dance with me, will you—"

"I don't believe we've met," Brad's voice cut in.

T. looked up, surprised, and Kelly took the opportunity to step back, out of his embrace. Beth's older sister was watching with unabashed interest as the two tall, blond men sized each other up.

"No, you're right," T. said. "We haven't met. I'm sorry, Kelly tends to…distract me."

"Oh, really?" Brad crossed his arms in front of him.

T. looked slightly surprised at the hostility in Brad's voice, and he glanced at Kelly as if looking for an explanation.

That's when it hit her.

T. Jackson didn't know that she and Brad were married. Kevin hadn't bothered to tell him.

"Are you gonna introduce us?" Brad asked her, a touch impatiently.

"Brad, this is Jackson Winchester," she said. "He was my brother's college roommate."

She looked up at T., who had held out a friendly hand toward Brad. The two men shook.

"T., I'd like you to meet Brad Foster," Kelly said. "My husband." For some mysterious reason, her eyes had suddenly filled with tears.

T. stared at her, an expression of shock clearly written across his usually unflappable face.

"Oh, God," he breathed. "You're married?"

She tried to smile. "Yeah."

"How could you be married?" he asked, disbelief in his voice. "You're only nineteen."

He reached out, pulling her chin up so he could look

into her eyes, as if he were hoping that something he saw there would prove her words wrong.

Brad stepped forward. "I'd appreciate it if you kept your hands off my wife."

T. Jackson let go of Kelly as if he'd been burned.

As she watched, tears formed in his eyes. He tried to blink them back. "I guess I missed your eighteenth birthday," he said softly.

Kelly nodded. "I guess you did."

"Oh, Kelly," he said.

She glanced back up into his eyes, and for one brief moment, he held her gaze, and she saw the white heat of his pain, the depth of his misery.

"Excuse me," T. whispered, and nearly ran from the room.

Brad stared after him. "People always have too much to drink at these things."

Kelly had spent the rest of the afternoon trying to convince herself that seeing T. hadn't really been that big a deal. Naturally she'd felt rattled; having him there had been a surprise. And as for the nearly over-powering urge to throw herself down on the floor and cry, well, that had had more to do with Brad's news that he'd found a job in California, than with anything else. Hadn't it...?

But as Kelly lay in the heat of the summer night nearly four years later, it all clicked into place.

She'd married Brad not because she loved him, but because he was so much like T. Jackson—or at least she thought he was—with his imposing height and blond hair. And even though she denied it, when she saw T. again at Kevin's wedding, deep down she re-alized the magnitude of her mistake.

Kelly stared at the ceiling, seeing T. as he had

looked at lunchtime today, walking down the city street, dressed down for comfort in the afternoon heat. She could see the tanned planes and angles of his handsome face as he sat across from her at the café table. She could see the longing in her own eyes, mirrored in the reflective lenses of his sunglasses.

There was no denying that she missed him.

She missed him following her around campus all day and all night, popping up in the most unexpected places to give her a lift or ask her out. She missed hearing his voice and talking to him. She missed the way he listened to her as if every word she said was of the utmost importance.

She missed his friendship, that much was clear.

But she couldn't deny that she missed him in other ways, too. When she saw him at lunch, her body had responded with astonishing speed to his nearness, and she walked away feeling utterly frustrated.

God, she still wanted him.

Aha, triumphantly cried the side of her that always played devil's advocate. I've been right all along. You *do* still love him.

Don't get carried away, she chastised herself. Lust and love don't always go hand in hand.

Still, as she lay awake into the late hours of the night, she could see T.'s stormy green eyes and hear an echo of his voice saying, *This is not over. I'm under your skin.*

Around two-thirty, Kelly fell into a restless sleep, only to dream about T. Jackson Winchester.

''So when are you going to call her?'' Jared asked. Jax was sitting in front of his computer, arms folded across his chest. A glance at his watch told him it was still not even nine o'clock in the morning.

It was going to be another hot one. He could already see heat waves shimmering out on the sandy beach.

Jax had a similar heat cooking inside of him at the thought of calling Kelly and hearing her voice. And if everything went according to plan, he'd be seeing her in only a few hours.

He would be using her ambition as a means to get her out here, though, to put her within his grasp. It felt like cheating, but Jax reminded himself that he had to do whatever it would take to get her to spend time with him.

"All's fair in love and war," Jared supplied helpfully. "So why don't you call her?"

"Why don't you quit trying to distract me?" Jax said. "I'm not going to call Kelly until nine, and I should probably even wait until ten. Right now I *should* be finishing this damned book, and *you* should be helping."

"Hey, *I'm* not the one who left me hanging here on the Boston Common with Carrie for two solid days." Jared was disgruntled. "And on top of all that, she's still mad at me. Why am I here? What's the purpose of this scene? Maybe you just want to torture me. I suppose that could be it. God knows you *love* to torture me—"

"This is where you notice the bruises on Carrie's face," Jax said, starting to write.

Horrified, Jared looked closer.

Carrie had tried to cover it with powder, but he could see the fading bruise beneath her eye and across her delicate cheekbone. She ducked her head, turning away.

"I have to go—"

Jared caught her arm. "Who did this to you?"

"I fell." She couldn't meet his gaze as she pulled away.

He swore sharply, but it was the sudden tears filling his eyes that slowed her feet. "Why do you stay with him, Carrie?" he asked. "Lord—how could you *marry* him—"

But as she wheeled to face him, it was anger, not sorrow that made her voice shake. "How dare you," she said. "How *dare* you come back here, and how *dare* you look at me as if I were the one who betrayed *you?* God *damn* you to hell, Jared Dexter. *You're* the one who deserted *me!* You *promised* you would come for me—"

"Why didn't you wait?" It came out a whisper filled with his anguish and pain. "You should have waited for me."

He held her by her shoulders, and as he stared down into her deep blue eyes he could see...fear?

"Let go of me," she said. "You're making a scene. If someone tells Harlan they saw me here like this with you—"

Jared released her, feeling sick.

Jared looked up at Jax. "I don't like where this is going."

"You're definitely not gonna like where Carrie's going."

"Going? As in *away?* No, don't tell me—"

"She and Harlan are headed out west," Jax said. "Yippee-yi-oh-ki-ay. They're buying a ranch in California."

"California?" Jared threw up his hands in disgust. "Are you sure this book is going to have a happy ending?"

"I'm sure of nothing these days," Jax replied.

"Lord save me from depressed writers." Jared rolled his eyes.

"Relax," Jax said. "It won't be long now 'til Part Three. Part Three is three years later."

"Three *years!* What have I been doing for three *years?*"

"Getting richer. Your business ventures keep earning you more money. Everything you touch turns to gold."

"Everything except my love life." Jared sulked.

"You go west," Jax said, and Jared stopped sulking.

"Okay. Things are starting to look better. Where exactly did you say Harlan Kent's ranch was?"

"I didn't." Jax sat back in his chair. "But it's near Los Angeles."

"So what's going to happen?" Jared was still suspicious.

"First you go to L.A.," Jax told him, "where you find out that Harlan's dead."

The hard planes of Jared's handsome face softened into a smile. "Now you're talking. You had me worried there for a while."

Jax pulled himself back to his computer keyboard, but Jared shook his head.

"It's after nine," he pointed out. "You should call Kelly."

"Just let me get this started," Jax said distractedly.

"You're stalling."

Jared was right. He *was* stalling. No more stalling.

With a click of his mouse, Jax cleared the computer screen.

Taking a deep breath, he turned and looked at the telephone, then glanced at his watch to be sure it really was past nine.

He picked up the phone and dialed Kelly's home number. It rang once. Twice. Three times. Four.

"Hello?" She was breathless, as if she'd run for the phone.

"Hey, Kel," Jackson said. "It's me. Jax. How are you?"

"Soaking wet, actually," she said in her familiar, husky voice. "I was just turning off the shower when I heard the phone. Can you hold on a sec while I dry off and grab my robe?"

A sudden vivid image of Kelly, standing with only a towel around her, took Jax's breath away. He almost couldn't answer. "Yeah, sure," he managed to say.

He heard the sound of the phone being put down and then silence for about thirty seconds. Then she was back.

"Sorry about that," she said.

"No problem." He wiped the sweat off his upper lip with the back of his hand.

"It's funny. I was just thinking about you."

In the shower? He shook his head. It wasn't going to do him any good to start thinking along those lines.

"What's up?" she asked.

Funny you should ask... He cleared his throat. "I read your manuscript. It's good."

There was silence.

"*You* read it." Another pause. "I thought Stefanie was going to."

Mentally Jax froze. God, of *course*. Kelly thought

that *Stef* was Jayne Tyler. She had no reason to think anything else. He realized that she was waiting for him to say something, that his silence was stretching longer and longer.

"Yeah," he finally said, hoping his next words would take her attention off the vagueness of his comment. "Look, your story could use some revisions. And that's why I'm calling. I thought you might be interested in letting Jayne Tyler help you with the rewrites."

It was his ace in the hole, his secret weapon, his only shot, and he prayed desperately that it would work.

"You're kidding."

"No."

More silence. He could almost hear the wheels turning in her head.

"Our offices are here at the house in Dennis," he said, mostly to fill the empty space. "I figure you could have the revisions done by the end of the summer."

"Dennis, huh?" She made a sound that might've been a laugh. "It's a hefty commute, considering I don't have a car."

"Um," Jax said. "There's plenty of room for you to stay over."

She laughed. "Now, how did I know you were going to say that?"

"Oh, come on, Kel." Jax closed his eyes and prayed. "Summer on the Cape…?"

"T., will you be honest with me?"

"I'll try."

"Is my writing really any good, or is this just a ploy to get me out to Cape Cod?"

"Yes, and yes," he admitted.

Kelly laughed. "Right," she said. "Okay, answer this one. What does Jayne get from doing this? I mean, I understand *your* motivation, but what's in it for her?"

"Whoa," Jax backpedaled. "Wait a minute. Kelly, this isn't some kind of sexual bribe. I don't want you to think that you owe me anything. I just want you to have a chance to get to know me again. That's all." He took a deep breath. "I'm not trying to buy your love. Or anything else. I'm just trying to get you out here. Once you're here, I'm hoping…you'll fall in love with me again."

"Well." Kelly was slightly breathless. "As long as we're being honest with each other, I have to tell you that I have no intention of falling in love with you *ever* again, Tyrone."

She'd already made that way more than clear. "I know. Will you come anyway?"

"What kind of computer do you have?"

"A PC," he said. "Why?"

"I knew it," she said. "More proof that we're not compatible. I've got a Mac. I better plan on bringing it."

Jax stood, twirled around in a silent dance of victory and then untangled himself from the phone cord. Yes. *Yes.*

"Can you pick me up?" she asked. "Or is that a stupid question?"

"Stupid question," he agreed. "Really stupid. I'll be there before noon. Don't forget to pack your bathing suit."

"Of course," Kelly said dryly. "I always wear my bathing suit when I write."

"Oh, come on. It's summer. This is Cape Cod. You can't *not* bring your bathing suit."

"I won't be packed by noon," Kelly warned him.

"I'll help you pack."

"I must be crazy."

"I promise you, Kelly," Jax said, "you won't regret this."

"I already regret this." But then she laughed. "I *am* crazy. See you later, T."

Jackson hung up the phone and let out a whoop that could be heard clear across the bay.

Chapter 11

"Rule number one," Kelly said, sitting in Jax's little sports car as they sped down Route 3 toward Cape Cod. "No touching."

"I can live with that." Jax smiled as he glanced at her. "With exceptions, of course—"

"No exceptions," she said sternly.

"Well, what if I have to pull you out of a burning building?" Jax asked. "Or push you out of the way of a speeding car? Or—"

"I don't intend to spend much time in burning buildings or near speeding cars this summer. Rule number two."

"All rules have exceptions," Jax told her stubbornly. "And you know it."

"Rule number two," Kelly repeated, crossing her arms. She could be just as stubborn. "No looking at me like you want to eat me for dinner."

Jax exhaled a loud burst of air as he laughed. "Like *what?*"

"You know what I mean."

"No, I *don't*—" He was *laughing* at her.

"Yes, you do." She smacked his arm.

"Uh-uh-uh. That was a direct violation of rule number one. No touching."

"You *know* the look I mean," Kelly insisted, choosing to ignore him. "It's like you're taking off my clothes with your eyes."

"Rule number two," Jax repeated. "No taking off your clothes with my eyes. It's gonna make it hard to undress you, considering rule number one. How about taking off your clothes with telekinesis? Is that permitted?"

Kelly couldn't hide her laughter, which was only serving to make him act sillier than ever. "T., you're not taking me seriously."

"On the contrary. I'm taking you extremely seriously." The road was flat and straight and empty, and he took his eyes off of it for a long moment to study her. Despite the car's air-conditioning, she was sticky and hot and—

"*That's* the look," she accused him. "You were giving me that look—"

Startled, Jackson pulled his eyes back to the road. "I was *not*—"

"Yes, you were."

"Well, if I was, I didn't know it. How can I stop doing something I don't do intentionally?"

"Wear your sunglasses."

"Day and *night?*" he said. "Inside the *house?*"

She shrugged. "Whatever works. Rule number three."

"There's more?"

"No sweet talk, no marriage proposals, no constant reminders that you want us to be more than friends, no sexual innuendos."

Jax sighed. "I'm not sure I'll be able to stand the pressure."

"Rule number four—"

"Kelly, you're not giving me an awful lot to work with here."

"No trying to distract me with your body."

"Excuse me? No trying to *what?*"

"No walking around half-naked," she elaborated. "You know."

"Kel, we're going to be living at a beach house," Jax said. "*Every*one walks around half-naked. Including you. I hope."

"Rule number five—No flirting." She looked over at him. "That's going to be a hard one for you. I don't think you're capable of communicating with a woman without flirting."

Jax was silent for a long time. Finally he looked over at her and lifted an eyebrow. "Every single way I could think of responding to that statement could be interpreted as flirting. You're right. I'm completely doomed."

He pulled off the highway and down to the end of the exit ramp. There were no cars behind him, so he put the car in park and turned toward Kelly.

"T. Jackson Winchester the Second's Only Rule." He had a dangerous glint in his eye and Kelly tried to back away, but there was nowhere to go. "Once a day," he told her, "every single day, I intend to break each and every one of your rules. Rules number one and two..." He touched the side of her face, pulling her chin up so that her gaze met his. He looked into her eyes, letting his desire for her simmer. "Rule number three," he whispered. "Kelly, I want to make love to you for days without stopping. Please, will you stop this nonsense and just marry me?"

"No," she breathed, caught in the turbulent green of his eyes. Oh, God, this was a mistake.

He leaned closer and kissed her, but instead of a passionate attack, his mouth was soft, sweet. "The kiss was a variation on rule four," he explained, then he smiled. "These rules are going to kill me. But frankly, I can't think of a better way to go."

She could kiss him. She could lean forward right now and kiss him, and, like the man said, stop this nonsense.

Instead, Kelly closed her eyes until she felt the car moving forward. She couldn't give in. She *wouldn't* give in.

Not unless she wanted him to break her heart all over again.

The Winchester house was enormous, and it sat on a craggy hill overlooking the beach. It was modern, with lots of odd angles and high ceilings. No single corner came together absolutely square.

The large living room was a few steps down from the entryway, and it had huge sliding glass doors that led out onto a wide wooden deck. The furniture looked surprisingly comfortable, and the room was decorated all in white and various shades of blue and green—the colors of the beach. There was a fireplace and an expensive sound system and a wall full of books. It was not the cold, imposing room that Kelly had expected from T.'s descriptions of the Winchester estates.

"Nice," she said.

T. laughed at the tone of her voice. "Why so surprised?"

She turned to face him, and caught a glimpse of her own rueful smile in the reflective lenses of his sunglasses. He was making a point to wear them inside the house. "Isn't this your parents' house?"

"Not anymore." He shifted the weight of her suitcase to his left hand. "I bought it from them a few years ago."

"But this *is* the house you lived in when you were in high school," Kelly said.

He smiled, setting the suitcase down. "This is it. Come on, I'll give you the grand tour."

She followed him back up the stairs and then up several more steps into the kitchen. It was huge and gleaming, with two different refrigerators, what seemed like miles of counter space and a center island that contained a second sink. All of the cabinets were made of a light knotted pine, and on the floor was cream-colored ceramic tile. Shining pots hung from a grid on one wall, and fruits and vegetables sat in baskets that dangled from the center beam.

"I keep a grocery list on the refrigerator," Jax told her. "If you want anything special, just add it to the list. I'll pick it up next time I'm at the store."

"I didn't know you could cook."

"I'm a whiz at grilled-cheese sandwiches," he said. "My other specialty is cornflakes. I pour a mean pitcher of milk."

Kelly followed him several steps down the hall. "This is the dining room." He didn't bother to go inside the large room that held a banquet-size table and about sixteen chairs. "But I don't use it. I eat out on the deck." He smiled. "Or in a restaurant. Usually in a restaurant."

He led her up a full set of stairs to the second floor. A long hallway stretched both right and left. He turned left. "This is my wing. It's over the garage." He pointed at several doors. "Guest bedroom, guest bedroom, bathroom. This is my office."

After peeking into the two very tastefully decorated guest rooms, Kelly followed T. Jackson into his office. It was a big room that, like the living room, overlooked the beach.

"I can move a desk in here for your computer," Jax said. "Or you can set it up in your room, whichever you prefer. Some people don't like writing when someone else is in the room, so…"

Kelly turned to him and smiled. "T., at school I work in the newsroom. If you don't mind, I'll put my computer in here. Unless you think having Stefanie and me working in here will disturb you?"

"Um…"

"What's in here?" Kelly curiously pushed open the door that connected his office to another room.

"My bedroom." He came to stand behind her, finally taking off his sunglasses.

His room was dark, with the shades still pulled down and the big bed unmade. Clothes were draped over chairs and in piles on the floor. His closet door was open, revealing a row of neatly hung shirts and jackets. The room was cool and dim and smelled good, like Jackson.

It wasn't hard to picture T. asleep in that bed, his hair tousled, his muscles relaxed.

His arms around her.

Kelly took a step back and bumped into him. Her entire back pressed against his entire front, and he put his arms around her to steady her. But he moved away almost immediately, giving her space.

"Sorry," she said.

His mouth twisted into a quick smile that didn't quite reach his eyes. "Hey, it's your rule. If it were up to me…"

Kelly followed his gaze back to his rumpled bed.

It wasn't hard to figure out what he was thinking. It would have been even easier to give in, to throw her arms around his neck and pull him toward that bed.

Kelly was suddenly very grateful that she had set up those rules, because she knew that if T. so much as touched her right now, her willpower would dissolve.

But he barely even glanced at her before putting his sunglasses back on. "I'll get the rest of your stuff in from the car. Why don't you pick which guest room you want to use? There's one more at the end of this hall, and three down on Stef's wing."

He disappeared, leaving Kelly still standing in the doorway to his bedroom. She looked back at his bed one more time, then quickly went into the hall. Moving down to the other side of the hall, Stefanie's wing, he had called it, she picked the room that was farthest away from T.'s.

It was decorated all in green. Green wallpaper, green bedspread, green curtains. There was a dresser and a rocking chair and a huge walk-in closet that was empty. The room also had its own bathroom. Maybe all the bedrooms did, Kelly thought suddenly, wondering at the value of a house this size, with all those bathrooms, *on* the beach.

As T. Jackson carried her suitcase in, he didn't comment on the geography of her room choice. He set her luggage on the floor and nodded toward the bed. "Did you know that's a water bed?"

Kelly looked at it in surprise. "No, I didn't." She sat down on the bed, and felt waves rolling back and forth inside the water-filled mattress. It was fun, kind of like an amusement park ride. She lay back on the bed, letting herself float.

She bounced higher as T. jumped onto the bed next to her. "My parents got it in the seventies," he said with a grin. "Needless to say, this is the room I slept in when I was in high school."

Kelly sat up, staring at him. "Forget this room. I can't stay in here. It's probably haunted with the ghosts of high school girlfriends past. I'd never get any sleep."

T. laughed, propping his head up on his hand, his arm bent at the elbow. "I never brought anyone home, because I didn't want to risk people finding out that I lived alone," he said. "Well, no, that's not entirely true. Mary Jo Matthews came over once. Uninvited, though. We went steady for about a month during my senior year. She dumped me for the captain of the football team."

"Ouch."

"I got over it."

Stretched out next to him on the gently rolling bed, she could remember him as an eighteen-year-old. No doubt all the girls in the school had sighed over him, some of them doing more than sighing.

"I'll bet you did," she said.

"If we had gone to high school together, I would've been scared to death of you."

"Why?" she asked.

"You were a math nerd, remember?" He grinned. "I really stank at math."

"I could've tutored you." God, why did she say that?

"I would've invited you over anytime."

"I think I'd rather have a room with a regular bed," Kelly said.

The water shifted as Jax stood, and the force of the internal waves knocked Kelly over. She laughed helplessly, trying to regain her balance.

Jax held out his hand to help her up, and she reached for it automatically. But he let go of her almost immediately, and she bounced back down onto the rolling surface of the water bed.

"Rule number one," he reminded her.

No touching.

Trying not to swear too loudly, Kelly scrambled for the edge of the bed and got herself back onto the steadiness of the floor.

T. had already carried her suitcase out of the room, and she went into the hall and watched him walk back down toward his wing.

"What's wrong with this room?" Kelly asked, stopping in front of the next closest guest room.

He glanced back at her. "That one doesn't have its own bathroom."

"And this room?" She pointed to the door directly across the hall.

"No bay view."

"Figures," she muttered, following him into a guest bedroom that was on the bay side of the house, one door down from his office, two doors down from his bedroom.

It was larger than the green room, with bigger windows and a bigger bathroom. The carpeting was a dusty rose, and the curtains and bedspread were white. Besides the double bed, the room held a dresser and a wicker chair.

T. Jackson put her suitcase down on the bed. "I'll bring your computer up to the office while you unpack."

Kelly followed him out into the hall again. "Hey," she said, and he turned around to look at her. At least she thought he was looking at her. It was hard to tell since he'd put his sunglasses back on.

"I don't want to unpack," she told him. "At least two years have passed since I've been within twenty miles of a beach. I'm going to go for a swim."

"Mind if I come along?"

Yes. No. Oh, brother, she didn't know what she wanted.

No, she knew *exactly* what she wanted. And what she wanted and what was good for her were two very different things.

What had she been thinking when she agreed to come and spend more than two months here with T.? Had she really thought she'd be able to come to Cape Cod and *not* wind up in bed with him? She couldn't be in the same room with him without wanting him. Heck, she couldn't be on the same continent, the same *planet* with him without wanting him.

But she had no intention of giving in to her desire. No, thank you. There was just no way she was going to risk letting him back into her heart. And if she let him get close to her in any way, he was bound to be able to break through her protection. And then she'd wind up hurt.

If T. cooperated and followed the rules she'd set down, that would be only half the battle. The other half was her own feelings, her own wants. Please, God, don't let me start sleepwalking, because my subconscious will surely lead me directly to T.'s bed.

Maybe it would be easier when Stefanie was here. After all, it was Stefanie she'd be working with day after day, not T.

Meanwhile, he was standing at the top of the stairs, watching her, waiting for her to answer his question.

"I'll meet you out on the deck," she finally said, and was rewarded by a quiet smile.

It was the quiet smiles that were the most dangerous.

She went into her room and tightly closed the door.

Kelly stood out on the restaurant patio, leaning on the rail, watching the sunset and drinking a beer. Despite all the sunblock she'd put on today, she'd gotten a slight sunburn, just enough to give her skin a tingling, sensitive feeling. In order to avoid the discomfort that a bra would cause, she had put on a sundress with a halter top.

At first she had hesitated, not wanting to give T. the wrong idea. In fact, for precisely that reason, she had intended to wear either jeans or shorts and T-shirts during her entire stay, but she had a particularly bright red stripe of sunburn at the edge of her bathing suit on her back, and the thought of pulling jeans or even shorts on over that was just too dreadful.

On the other hand, if she'd intended to only wear androgynous, casual clothes while she was here on the

Cape, then why had she even packed this sundress in the first place? Or the three other skirts and dresses she'd brought?

"Am I allowed to tell you how beautiful you look?"

She turned to see T. standing next to her.

"Or is that against the rules?" He leaned next to her against the railing, taking a sip from his own glass of beer.

"I think you already managed to tell me." She stared out at the water. "And, yes, it's against the rules. But thank you, anyway."

"Oh, now, wait. If I'm going to break a rule, I'm going to do it right." He looked at her, letting his eyes caress her face. "You're incredibly lovely," he told her. "Your beauty rivals the sunset and—"

Kelly laughed. "Oh, ack."

"Ack?" he repeated, eyebrows elevated. "I'm waxing poetic, and all you can say is ack?"

"Rule six—No waxing poetic. Especially not on an empty stomach. Speaking of empty stomachs, are we going to eat sometime this century by any chance?"

"It shouldn't take more than another ten minutes." Jax sighed melodramatically. "I remember a time when food didn't matter to you, when my kisses were sufficient nourishment."

"Yeah, well, I'm on a diet, remember?" Kelly countered.

"Just let me know when you're ready for a little bingeing," Jax said.

"Tyrone," she said, all kidding pushed aside. "You promised. I'm not going to stick around if I have to fight you off for the rest of the summer."

"So stop fighting," Jackson's eyes were equally

grave. ''Surrender, Kel. I guarantee you won't regret it.''

The breeze ruffled his blond hair and he carelessly pushed it out of his face as he watched her.

Surrender. She could imagine how good it would feel right now to lean back against his chest and watch the sunset with his arms wrapped around her. She could imagine the way his breath would feel against her neck as he leaned close to whisper soft, seductive words to her—

''Winchester. Table for two,'' a voice announced.

Saved.

Not that she had any intention of actually surrendering, Kelly told herself as she followed the hostess through the restaurant to the small, lantern-lit table at the railing of a covered open deck. She slid into her seat, watching as T. Jackson somehow managed to squeeze his long legs into the small space opposite her.

''Please, will you ask the waitress to bring us a couple of bowls of clam chowder right away?'' T. asked the hostess as she handed them their menus. He smiled across the table at Kelly. ''My friend here is starving. I don't want her to start eating the tablecloth.''

Kelly could see the bold interest in the woman's eyes as she smiled down at T. Well, sure, why not? T. had to be the best-looking man in the place. Kelly was getting quite a number of envious glances from other women. But if he noticed, he was hiding it well. To look at him, anyone would think he was oblivious to everyone in the restaurant besides Kelly.

Another woman might've been flattered, or made to feel special by his undivided attention. But not her, no way. In fact, she'd prefer it if he found someone else to look at that way.

He was being careful to keep that hot, hungry, gobble-her-up look from his eyes, but this soft, faintly amused adoration was unbearable in its own way.

The soup came out almost right away, and T. soon gave some of his attention to eating. As they ate, and throughout the rest of dinner, he kept the conversation light and almost pointedly not flirtatious.

Kelly felt herself relax.

Jax felt himself start to sweat. He wasn't sure how long he could keep up the big-brother act.

Somehow he'd managed to spend three and a half hours on the beach with Kelly without breaking any of her damned rules. Despite the fact that her bathing suit was a chlorine-faded one-piece, she *did* look good enough to eat. And watching her rub sunblock onto her long, slender legs...

God, he was in trouble here.

Jax couldn't wait until tomorrow, until he could break her rules again. What was that expression? Go big or stay home. Maybe tomorrow he'd break those rules in a big way. Like by crawling into bed with her in the morning.

Inwardly he laughed, imagining the expression on her face.

On the other hand, he didn't want to push so far that she'd go running back to Boston.

How was he going to live through the rest of tonight? How could he continue to sit here and pretend that Kelly didn't own his heart?

Worst of all, how was he going to tell her the truth about Jayne Tyler? He had to tell her. Tonight.

As the busboys cleared the table, as the waitress brought out mugs of coffee, Jax was silent, staring out at the darkness that had fallen over the water. How was Kelly going to react to his news?

She was probably going to be angry, upset maybe, annoyed at the very least. She might think that he had purposely tricked her, purposely lied to her.

Jax considered waiting until they got home to tell her, but figured maybe if he told her in public, here at the restaurant, she might not yell at him quite as loudly.

She met his eyes as she took a sip of her coffee.

"You're so quiet," she said. "What are you thinking about?"

This was it. The perfect opportunity. "I have a secret I've got to tell you."

Kelly stopped drinking and slowly put her mug down. He could tell that she was thinking carefully, trying to decide what her response should be. He didn't give her time to say anything.

"I haven't told anyone," he said. "Ever. Not in the three years since—well, it's been four, really."

Kelly watched him as the light from the lantern on the table flickered across his face and reflected the shiny gold of his hair. What kind of secret could it possibly be? She was curious and a little worried. He looked so serious, so solemn.

"Well, Stefanie knows," T. said, then smiled. "She'd have to know. I mean, of course she knows."

Kelly hadn't said a word. She just sat there, watching him, the soft light playing across her beautiful face. Her eyes were dark and almost colorless in the dimness, and her hair curled slightly in the damp ocean air.

"I'm not sure I really want to know what this secret is," she said finally. "But I'm dying of curiosity. What'd ya do, T.? Kill somebody? Rob a bank? Run for office? Have an illegitimate child? What?"

T. Jackson laughed. He was fooling with the container that held little packs of sugar for coffee, and the salt and pepper shakers that were in the center of the table. His large, strong fingers toyed with them nervously.

Nervously. If T. was so nervous that it showed, if he was *that* nervous about telling her whatever this secret was, then it must be serious. Kelly swallowed. Was it his health? Was he sick? She remembered how terrible he'd looked at Kevin's wedding. That was just about four years ago, wasn't it?

Even though she knew she shouldn't touch him, Kelly reached across the table and took T.'s hand, lacing her fingers with his. He looked up at her, his eyes momentarily opened wide in surprise. For that one instant, he was stripped of all his pretense of ease and his self-assuredness. His face looked younger, more vulnerable.

This was the same T. Jackson she'd had a glimpse of the night she'd gone to his hotel room with him. She'd seen that same look in his eyes the second time he'd made love to her that night. She hadn't thought they'd be able to surpass their first explosive joining, but T. had made love to her again so slowly, so unhurriedly, so sensually, the memory could still leave her feeling weak. And as she had gazed up into his eyes, as he had touched her, caressed her, filled her, it had been as if he let her see into his soul.

Now he looked down at her hand intertwined with his and smiled.

"Tell me," she said, squeezing his hand gently.

Jax looked into the depths of Kelly's eyes, carefully hiding the surge of triumph that he felt. She cared about him enough to take his hand. She cared about him enough to worry that this secret was something serious. She cared—

Great. Inwardly he shook his head with disgust as the triumphant feeling vanished as quickly as it came. She had cared enough to break one of her rules—no touching—and that was a step forward, that was real progress in his fight to win her back, but as soon as he told her the truth, she was going to take about twenty-five giant steps back. Toward Boston, no doubt.

"Kel." He wondered if there was some easier way to tell her this. "I'm really…"

She was waiting.

Crap. "No, it's nothing."

"T.!" She let go of his hand, her eyes lit with exasperation.

Now that she wasn't touching him, it was easier. He didn't have to be afraid she would release his hand when he told her, because she already had.

"You're really *what?*" she asked, her steady gaze giving him no quarter.

"Whom." He smiled weakly. "It's not a what, it's a whom."

She blinked. Then laughed. Then pinned him to the seat with a look of disbelief. "Don't tell me. Don't you dare say this is some kind of secret identity or alter ego thing."

"Yes," T. said, and Kelly knew that he wasn't kidding by the amount of guilt she could see in his eyes. "That's it exactly."

Kelly pushed her coffee away, reaching instead for the half-full glass of white wine that she hadn't finished with her dinner. She took a calming sip and slowly put the long-stemmed glass back down. For several long moments she studied the light from the lantern as it shone through the wine, before she looked back at T.

"Are you trying to tell me that you're, like... *Bat*man?" she said, one eyebrow raised.

Jax laughed. "Close." He braced himself. "I'm Jayne Tyler."

She stared at him in shock. Gee, maybe a superhero would've gone over better, Jax thought.

"You're... *what?*"

"Whom," he said gently. "Jayne. Tyler. She may have my sister's face on the book covers, but the words are all mine."

He looked down at his mug of coffee, resisting the urge to shut his eyes tightly against the accusations he was so sure were going to follow.

But Kelly didn't make any accusations. She laughed.

Jax looked up at her.

"You're not kidding, are you?" She was smiling at him.

Wordlessly he shook his head no.

"I can't believe it." She laughed again. "I mean, I *do* believe it, and *wow!* I'm so proud of you, T. You're a writer, a *real* writer, an author. My God, Jayne Tyler is so good. I mean, *you're* so good! Where did you learn to write like that?"

She was still smiling at him, her eyes sparkling with enthusiasm. She wasn't angry. She was...*proud* of him? Jax fought the urge to lean across the table and kiss her.

"You're not mad at me?" he asked.

Kelly shook her head. "No," she said. "Well, maybe a little disappointed that you didn't trust me enough to tell me before this."

"I haven't seen an awful lot of you since I started writing," Jax pointed out. "This is the first time we've really had a chance to talk."

"Uh-oh." Sudden realization dawned. "This means I'm going to be working with *you* all summer, huh?"

Surrender. The word came immediately to mind as Kelly looked into the stormy gray-green of T.'s eyes. She'd only spent half a day with him, and already she was considering giving in. She could picture them working together during the day, taking breaks out in the sun on the beach, sharing a quiet, candlelit dinner like this every night and then going home to share T.'s bed. She could picture him kissing her. On the beach, in his office, in the car on the way home from dinner... With very little effort, she could picture them making love.

Kelly swallowed. There was a time not so very long ago when a summer like that would've been a dream come true. She had loved T. so much back then. She would have given herself to him for the summer, believing that the summer would last forever. But if there was one thing the past had taught her, it was that nothing lasted forever.

"Is the thought of working with me so terrible?" T. asked softly.

"No," she said, meeting his eyes. It wasn't. And that's what alarmed her. God help her. If she was with him all the time, she might actually start to believe him when he said that he loved her, that he wanted to marry her. And if she started to believe him, God knows she'd only end up hurt.

Kelly said good-night to T. out in the hall, leaving him standing there as she went into her room and carefully locked the door behind her.

Surrender.

Instead, she kicked off her shoes, went into her bathroom and brushed her teeth. She pulled down the shades and stepped out of her dress, gently rubbing lotion onto her sunburned skin. The big T-shirt she slept in was still in her suitcase, so she rummaged for it, then put it on, wincing as it hit her shoulders.

When they got home from dinner, T. had found a note from Stefanie on the kitchen table. She had left on a cruise to Alaska with Emilio. She wouldn't be back until the first week of August.

Kelly and T. Jackson were alone in this big house. It smelled like a setup, but Jackson swore he knew nothing about Stef's plans.

Right.

As she went to pull the white spread off the big bed, she saw an envelope resting on one of the pillows. Curious, she picked it up. The flap wasn't sealed, and she pulled out a single sheet of heavy bond paper and unfolded it.

It was a letter. From T. From his computer's laser printer.

Dear Kelly,

If it were up to me, I'd be in there with you right now. Instead I'm sitting in my office, staring out the window at the night, burning for your touch.

I want you.

I want to feel your lips on mine, your body against me. I want to entangle myself with you, bury myself, lose myself in you.

It is such heaven and such hell having you close enough to touch—

But we're playing by your rules.

So I'm not going to speak the words that are always on the tip of my tongue and constantly tell you how much I love you. I'm not going to show you how much by holding you in my arms and making love to you, the way I want to.

But I am going to write down the words I long to say, hoping that you'll read them, giving me at least a fighting chance to win back your heart.

He had signed it with his bold handwriting. *"I love you. Love, T."*

Kelly carefully folded the letter and put it back into the envelope. She turned off the light but lay awake for a long time before finally falling asleep.

Chapter 12

When Kelly got back from her morning run on the beach, T. Jackson wasn't in the house. On her way into the kitchen, she glanced out the window and saw that his sports car was gone from the driveway.

There was an envelope with her name on it on the kitchen table and, drinking directly from a half full bottle of seltzer that she'd pulled from the refrigerator, she opened it.

Another of T.'s letters. Love letters, she guessed she could call them. Since she'd arrived over a week ago, he'd left at least a dozen of them around for her to read. She hadn't even acknowledged them, and *he* certainly didn't bring up the subject.

It was as if he were two very different people. One was the good old friend who was helping her rewrite her novel, helping her straighten out the problems with her hero's motivation. The other was this ardent lover who had no shame when it came to writing his desires and passions, all of which involved her.

In this latest note, he described in extremely specific detail just how he wanted to kiss her when he returned home from the errands he was on.

Kelly felt her pulse increase as she read his words. It was scary to know that he was going to kiss her sometime today or tonight. Part of her was really looking forward to that kiss, and knowing *that* scared her even more.

As T. had promised that very first day, he broke all of her rules once a day, and only once a day. He would kiss her, tell her he loved her, ask her to marry him. She was never sure just when during the day that romantic attack was going to come. Several times it had happened first thing in the morning, but other days he had waited until afternoon or even after dinner. As a result, she was kept on edge almost all the time. And even after he kissed her, she found herself anticipating the next day's onslaught.

She also looked forward to his letters. And as much as she realized he was using them to break down her resolve not to get involved with him, she couldn't stop herself from reading them, sometimes over and over again.

Kelly took this latest letter back onto the deck with her and sat down on the steps as she finished the seltzer. Wow, it was going to be another megahot day. She wasn't even going to bother to shower. At least not before she put on her bathing suit and went into the bay for a swim.

She leaned her head back against the banister, feeling the hot sun on her face. She needed to put more sunblock on, or her fair skin was going to burn again.

She'd probably already sweated off the stuff she'd applied earlier this morning.

"Hey."

Kelly jumped, opening her eyes and turning to see T. Jackson standing by the sliding glass doors into the living room.

"Morning," he said. He already had on his neon-green bathing suit with an Amnesty International T-shirt on top. Don't Discount The Power Of The Written Word his shirt proclaimed in large block print. Write A Letter, Save A Life. Kelly glanced down at the letter she still held in her hands. The power of the written word, indeed.

"I picked up some groceries." T. looked at her over the top of his sunglasses. "Wanna help me unload the car?"

Kelly hauled herself to her feet. "Sure."

He stepped back to let her go through the door first, and she glanced up nervously as she passed within inches of him. But his face was relaxed, he was smiling. She couldn't see his eyes through the dark lenses of his sunglasses.

"How far did you run?" he asked.

"About three miles." She took a detour to put the empty seltzer bottle and the letter down on the kitchen counter. God, she wished he would just kiss her and get it over with. "I've got to start getting up earlier," she added. "It's getting too hot, even first thing in the morning. As soon as we're done here, I'm going for a swim."

Jackson pushed open the screen door and went out onto the driveway, where his car was parked.

The trunk was open wide and filled with cloth grocery bags. T. was environmentally correct. Somehow the realization didn't surprise her.

"I got you a present," he said.

"Fudge ripple ice cream?" Kelly lifted two of the bags out of the car and lugged them back toward the kitchen.

"I thought you outgrew that when you were fifteen." Jax carried two bags in each hand.

"Yeah, well, I've regressed." She tried to ignore the way the muscles in his arms and shoulders flexed as he almost effortlessly lifted the weight of all four bags up onto the kitchen table.

With an easy underhanded throw, he tossed her a small bag that bore the label of a local fashion boutique. "I bought you a new bathing suit."

Kelly looked from the bag she had caught to Jackson and back to the bag. "If it fits in this little bag, something tells me I'm not going to be eating much fudge ripple ice cream in the near future."

When she looked up again, T. was standing directly in front of her, and she knew from the look in his eyes that he was going to kiss her.

"Oh, T., yuck, I'm all sweaty." She tried to sidle away from him along the edge of the kitchen counter.

But he put his hands against the countertop, one on either side of her, penning her in. "I want to marry you, remember? For richer or poorer, for better or for worse... I don't think there's an exception for sweaty." With one finger, he caught a bead of perspiration that was dripping down past her ear. "Actually, it's kind of a turn-on."

Leaning forward, he smiled into her eyes and then he kissed her.

The bag with the bathing suit dropped to the floor

as Kelly was surrounded by T. Jackson. His fingers left trails of fire where he touched her, his mouth met hers with a blaze of heat.

"Marry me, Kelly." His breath was hot as he whispered into her ear.

But she pulled free of his arms, and this time he let her get away. "No. I'm sorry." It was the same answer she'd given him every day since she'd arrived.

And just like every day, it didn't faze him. Cheerfully he bent down and picked up the bag she'd dropped and handed it to her. With a smile, he went back to the car for another load of shopping bags.

How could he do it? Every day she wondered how he could kiss her like that one minute, then act as if everything were completely platonic the next. Kelly always felt as if she needed a few hours to recover.

She waited for her pulse to return to near normal, then slowly opened the bag. A bikini. Black and very tiny, although allegedly it *was* her size. She held it up, looking at it skeptically.

T. came back into the kitchen carrying the last of the groceries. "I figured you needed a new bathing suit," he said as he started to unload the groceries. He looked at her and smiled. "That one-piece you have is on the verge of becoming transparent when it's wet. Do you know they actually make bathing suits these days designed to do that?"

Kelly stuffed the bikini back into the bag. "You don't *really* expect me to believe you, do you?"

"Scout's honor. They were totally see-through. I saw 'em in a catalog. It was this amazing catalog with—"

"I meant about my bathing suit," she interrupted. "It's not *that* old."

He looked up from loading liter bottles of seltzer into the refrigerator. "Hey, *I'm* not going to complain if you want to wear a see-through bathing suit, Kel. I just thought you might want to be warned. If you don't believe me, try it on and step into the shower. You'll see."

Jax found Kelly in the office, hard at work. The windows were open wide and all the fans in the room were on and it was still hot.

"I thought you were going for a swim," he said.

She didn't look up from her computer. "I changed my mind and took a shower instead."

He grinned. "You tried on your old bathing suit, and you found out that I was right."

"All right. Fine." Kelly turned around and sighed. "Go ahead and say it."

"Say what?"

"I told you so."

But he didn't say anything. He just looked at her. Kelly quickly turned around. Damn. She knew she shouldn't wear this halter top, but even the thought of putting on a T-shirt on a day this hot was too unbearable.

"I'm almost done with these revisions," she announced, making her voice as businesslike as possible. "Actually, I *am* done, I'm just inputting the changes. It shouldn't take more than an hour or two."

"Good," Jax said. "I haven't worked on my novel all week. That'll give me some time to touch base with my characters. After lunch we can work on fixing up your love scenes."

Kelly cringed. "Do we have to?"

"Well, no. We don't *have* to. But you'll never sell your book if we don't."

"I guess when you put it that way…"

Jax sat at his computer, waiting the few seconds it took his word processing program to boot up. He popped in his Jared disk and quickly read through the last chapter that he'd written.

Jared was out in California, in Los Angeles. He'd bought himself a horse, a big black stallion, and he was riding out toward the ranch Carrie and her husband, Harlan, had bought nearly three years ago. He'd just found out that Harlan had died some months ago from a fever.

Jax started to write.

As Jared rode the trail, it was clear the entire area was having one hell of a drought. Dust rose up from the ground, covering his dark suit, making him cough. He tied his handkerchief around his mouth and nose, and pushed the wide brim of his hat down a little lower.

"Yo, so that's Kelly, huh?" Jared said. "Lord, will you look at those *legs!* Oh, baby!"

"Shut up," Jax muttered.

"I didn't say anything," Kelly said.

Jared laughed, his dark eyes sparkling with amusement. "This is great. Finally I can get the last word in. If you talk to me, Kelly's gonna think you're bonkers. And she'll be right. Man, she's beautiful. No wonder you've been so distracted. She's *hot.* I bet you're dying to kiss those shoulders—"

Jax scowled and started writing again.

He saw the dust kicked up by the running horses before he heard the familiar sound of their hooves on the hard-packed ground. Taking his rifle from the back of his saddle, he stuck the heels of his boots into his stallion's sides. The beast reared up on his hind legs, then launched like a Chinese rocket.

Jared saw sunlight reflecting off the barrels of at least four guns as he glanced over his shoulder. Four horses, four riders, four guns. Damned if he knew what they wanted. Damned if he was going to find out.

They fired their first shot at him when he was within eyesight of the gate of the Double K ranch. Carrie's ranch. The bullet zinged just over his head.

Jared took the turn in to the Double K at a dangerous speed, the big horse scrambling for a foothold in the loose dirt.

"There better be a good reason for this," Jared shouted. "If this is just some kind of stupid punishment, I'm going to be very, very annoyed."

"There's a good reason for everything I do," Jax muttered.

"Did you say something?" Kelly asked.

Jax looked up, meeting her inquisitive gaze. "Just arguing with my main character."

"Ah." She turned back to her own computer.

"I can't *believe* you actually told her," Jared said.

"She took that rather well," Jax murmured.

Kelly laughed. "T., do you do this all the time?"

"Do what?"

"Talk to yourself?"

"Hah! See, now she thinks you're nuts," Jared said.

"Do you think I'm nuts?" Jax asked Kelly.

"Are you really having a conversation with your main character?" she countered.

"I'm afraid so," he admitted. "Right now he's on the back of a galloping horse, with four men chasing and shooting at him. He's not very happy with me."

"I don't blame him. If you put me in that situation, I'd argue with you, too." Kelly laughed. "Why don't you stop arguing and just write the end of the scene, get him out of there?"

"Did you hear that?" Jax said to Jared. "Stop arguing."

The stallion was still running like a demon out of hell as he approached the ranch house and the barn. With his rifle in his hand, Jared tried to rein in the big horse, even as he turned to double-check that the four gunmen hadn't followed him this far.

A shot rang out, and Jared felt a tug of pain in his right arm. The rifle clattered onto the dry ground. Damn, he was bleeding and his arm hurt like the devil. He turned, trying to figure out where that gun had been fired from when a clear voice said, "Keep your hands up where I can see them."

Jared nudged his horse, who obligingly turned to face the owner of both the voice and the gun. With his left hand, he swept his hat off of his head.

"Hello, Carrie," he said.

Jax saved the job, cleared the screen, stood and stretched.

"I'm going to get a cup of coffee," he said. "You want something?"

"Are you talking to me or your imaginary friend?" Kelly asked.

"Very funny," Jax said.

"How'd you end that scene?" she asked.

"It was an obvious solution. I had the heroine shoot the hero."

Kelly laughed. "Did it shut him up?"

"Not a chance."

Kelly sat out on the deck, eating a salad for lunch. She heard the screen on the sliding door open and close, heard Jackson's bare feet as he approached. The heavy wooden deck chair groaned slightly under his weight as he sat down, and there was a soft hiss of escaping carbonation as he opened a can of soda.

She glanced at him, and he smiled at her from behind his sunglasses. He'd taken off his T-shirt, and as she tried not to watch, he rubbed sunscreen onto his broad shoulders.

"You know, we can work out here this afternoon," he said. "You're not really ready to start rewriting. We have to talk about the scene first, and we can just as easily do that out here as inside."

Kelly closed her eyes. She was going to sit here and talk about rewriting the love scenes in her book with this man who clearly wanted to have a physical relationship with her. Add into the confusion the fact that she and T. *had* made love not so many weeks ago, and it had been the best sex she'd ever had in her life. To top it all off, her hormones wanted more, particularly when T. sat around half-naked the way he was, like some bronzed, blond sun god.

Kelly sighed. "All right. Start by telling me what I did wrong."

"For one thing," Jax said, "the scene's too short. It's over too soon. Essentially you've been building up to this scene, you've been building up to your characters making love since page one. Your readers are going to feel disappointed if you don't give 'em their money's worth."

Kelly put her salad bowl down on the deck and picked up T.'s soda can. Caffeine-free cola. Good, she didn't think she could stand a jolt of caffeine right now. "Can I have a sip?"

He nodded, still watching her.

She took a long drink of the sweet liquid. It wasn't as cool as she'd expected. The hot sun had already warmed the aluminum can.

"So, okay." She felt a trickle of perspiration drip between her breasts as she handed the soda can back to T. "How many more pages am I going to have to write?"

"It's not a matter of pages," T. said. "I've read great love scenes that were only one page long. I've also read at least one that was twenty-two pages—"

Kelly stared at him. "Twenty-*two?* Pages? Of sex?" She laughed. "I don't think my thesaurus has that many synonyms for the word *passionately.*"

"Relax. I'm not telling you to write twenty-two pages. Five or six should be fine—"

"Five or *six?* I ran out of things to describe after two paragraphs." The sun was beating down on her. She could feel herself starting to burn. "Can I use some of your lotion?"

T. sat up, his muscles rippling. "Feelings, Kel."

She looked at him. "What?"

He dragged his chair closer to hers, sitting on the edge of it, his elbows resting on his knees. "It's not enough simply to describe who's on top, and who's kissing whom and where."

Kelly felt her cheeks getting warm.

"You should use the actual physical descriptions of the sex to reveal more about your characters," T. Jackson continued. "Do they take it slowly, take their time, or do they tear each other's clothes off? How they do it, particularly the first time, can say a lot about them."

Kelly looked up at T., remembering how they had made love that first time in his hotel room. Oh, boy, that had been explosive.

He looked at her for a moment over the top of his sunglasses, and she could tell from his eyes that he was thinking about that night, too. What did that night reveal about her own character? Kelly wondered. What did it say about the intensity of her feelings for him, that she was willing to make love to him so wildly, abandoning all conventions, ignoring all proprieties?

Not feelings, she corrected herself quickly. What she had with T. had nothing to do with feelings. It was all attraction. All good old-fashioned lust.

Are you sure? that voice in her head asked.

"But that physical description shouldn't be your main focus," T. said as he handed her the bottle of suntan lotion. He took off his sunglasses and gently set them down on the deck next to his can of soda.

Kelly put some lotion into her hand and carefully applied it to her face as he stood.

"You've got to get inside your characters' heads," he said as he walked behind her deck chair.

She turned, surprised, to look back at him as he pushed the big wooden chairback up slightly, releasing the frame from the bar that held it in place.

He smiled at her as he lowered her chair into a more reclined position. "You've got to tell the reader exactly what the characters are feeling."

He leaned over the back of the chair and gently took the bottle of suntan lotion from Kelly's hand. He squeezed some out onto his palm. "And I'm not just talking about physical sensations," he added, looking down at her with a small smile, "although they're good, too."

She pulled her gaze away from him and sat up with her arms tightly hugging her knees. She felt him sit down on the edge of her chair, slightly behind her, and she looked back at him, startled.

He began rubbing the suntan lotion onto the top of her shoulders and her bare back, and she inhaled sharply. The lotion was cool against her hot skin, but it was the touch of his hands that sent chills down her spine.

"It's how your character feels about the person who's touching her that's important," T. continued softly. She could feel his warm breath against her ear as he rubbed a generous amount of lotion down her arm. "Think about it. Your character could get touched exactly the same way by a friend and then by a lover. It could be a handshake, or an embrace, or maybe…maybe someone—a friend, or a lover—is putting suntan lotion on her back."

T. stopped to squeeze more lotion out onto his hand. Kelly turned toward him. "T.—"

"Relax," he said. "And pay attention. Maybe you'll learn something."

He reached behind her and began rubbing the lotion onto her other shoulder. Right, thought Kelly. If she was going to learn anything from this, it was that she liked T. Jackson's touch way too much. And she already knew that.

"So what's the difference?" T. said as if he hadn't been interrupted, as cool and collected as if he were giving a lecture from behind a podium instead of working the lotion down her other arm. "It's in the way your character feels for the person she's being touched by. It's her emotion that can make a simple, innocent caress—" he ran his fingers lightly back up her arm "—outrageously erotic."

Kelly closed her eyes, feeling her insides turn to jelly. No, she did *not* love this man, she told herself. It was just the sun, the heat, making her light-headed.

"The same theory applies in a love scene when the hero, the man your character loves, undresses her." With one deft pull, T. untied the top knot of her halter.

"T.!" Kelly caught the fabric before it fell forward, modestly holding it up against her breasts.

"I didn't want to get any lotion on your top," he explained as she felt his hands on the back of her neck. Wow, that felt good. She closed her eyes again, swallowing her words of protest.

"Your character would have a very different reaction if a stranger walked up and started undressing her," T. continued. "But there's no embarrassment with a lover, only—" his voice lowered slightly "—anticipation." His hand slipped around to her neck, her throat, as he rubbed lotion into her hot skin. He spread the cool, sweet-smelling cream down, lower, covering her collarbone and the tops of her breasts.

Jackson could feel Kelly's heartbeat underneath his hand. He could feel the rapid rise and fall of her chest. Even beneath the loose folds of the fabric that covered her full breasts, he could see the hard buds of her nipples. He was dying to touch all of her, to kiss her, suckle her. This was torture. He smiled wryly. But it was the best kind of torture he'd ever experienced.

He stood, and her eyes opened as he gently pressed her shoulders back against the lounge chair. Nudging her hips over slightly, he now sat facing her. She watched, wide-eyed, as he spread suntan lotion onto her stomach, onto the wide strip of soft skin that was between her halter and the waistband of her shorts.

Kelly stared up into T. Jackson's eyes. How could he be so cool and calm when she was about to have a heart attack? She'd been long reduced to a puddle of desire, and he was sitting there smiling at her as if they were discussing the weather.

She saw it then. One lone bead of perspiration traveling down the side of T.'s face, next to his ear. He *was* rattled. He was just very, very good at hiding it.

But it was as if somehow he knew he'd given himself away. His eyes flooded with heat as he slid the tips of his fingers down below the loose waistband of her shorts. Kelly stopped breathing as his gaze locked with hers. He leaned forward, as if he was going to kiss her, closer, closer, until his mouth was just a whisper away from her lips.

"Foreplay," he whispered, his breath warm and sweet against her face. "When you write a good love scene, you've got to have plenty of foreplay. It's all part of the anticipation."

He straightened up without kissing her, but his eyes held hers as he said, "And if you do it right, most of the love scene can take place while your characters still have their clothes on."

He turned slightly then and squeezed a long, white line of suntan lotion first on one of her legs and then the other, from the tops of her thighs all the way down to her instep. Starting at her feet, he used both hands to rub the lotion into her skin.

His hands moved up her leg at a leisurely, deliberate pace. It was shockingly sensuous, and unbelievably delicious. Kelly opened her mouth but couldn't find the words to stop him. Truth was, she didn't *want* to stop him.

"If you do it right—" T.'s voice was low now, like a caress "—one look, or a simple touch between lovers, can be as intimate as making love. But you've got to reveal what your characters are feeling."

His eyes were smoky gray-green as he looked at her, and now there was no hiding the sheen of perspiration on his forehead and upper lip. Kelly could see his pulse beating hard in his neck. His face held undisguised hunger as his fingers lingered on the soft skin on the inside of her thigh. The lotion had been long since rubbed in, but still he didn't pull his hands away.

"Imagine," he said, his voice husky, "if you loved me."

This was it. He was going to kiss her. And then they were going to make love, and she wasn't going to protest. She wasn't going to say one word. She couldn't. Not even if her life had depended on it.

But he didn't kiss her.

Instead, he reached for her hand, and taking it, he

brushed her palm lightly with his thumb, drawing circles on the sensitive skin, round and round. "Imagine how you would feel," he whispered. "Imagine the *emotions* you'd feel just from a simple touch."

Kelly stared up at Jax. Emotions. Imagine the emotions. She must have one heck of an imagination, because those imaginary emotions were damn near bowling her over.

He put the bottle of suntan lotion into her hand. "That's what it's really about. Love and emotion. Try rewriting your scene, focusing on what your characters are feeling in their hearts. You'll write a lot more than two paragraphs. I can guarantee it."

He stood, put his sunglasses on and walked calmly down the steps, heading for the cool water of the bay.

Kelly watched him until he was out of sight.

Imagine if you loved me.

She didn't have to imagine. She just had to remember.

And that wasn't very hard to do at all.

Chapter 13

The morning dawned hazy and humid.

After spending the evening writing and rewriting the first love scene in her book, Kelly had had a restless sleep. The setting sun had lowered the record high temperatures by only a few degrees, and the night had been almost impossibly hot.

Never mind the fact that she couldn't stop thinking about the way T. Jackson's hands had felt as he had spread suntan lotion on her legs.

She'd skip her run this morning, take a nice, cool swim instead.

It was a good plan, until she got onto the beach and found T. already sitting there.

"Good morning," he greeted her.

"What are you doing up so early?" she asked suspiciously.

T. shrugged. "Too hot to sleep." He was wearing the same neon-green bathing suit he'd had on yesterday. His hair was wet, and water beaded on his muscular body. He'd already been in for a swim.

It was a new day, Kelly realized, looking down at him. It was a new day, and sometime today he was going to kiss her. Her stomach knotted in anticipation.

As Jax watched, Kelly put her towel down on the sand chair next to his and kicked off her sandals. With one big yank, she pulled her T-shirt over her head.

She was wearing the black bikini. God, she looked fabulous. He grinned his appreciation, but she ignored him.

Jax followed her down to the edge of the ocean, watching as she walked directly into the water until it covered all but her shoulders. He crash-dived in, surfacing near her. Shaking his wet hair out of his face, he moved closer.

"Couldn't you at least have picked out a bathing suit that had more *suit* to it?" she asked, backing away.

"But you look so good in black," T. said as innocently as possible as he moved toward her.

"Where's the black?" Kelly asked. She kept backing away, heading for the beach, exposing more and more of the bathing suit in question to the open air. "When I looked in the mirror, all I could see was skin."

"You look good naked, too. The combination is...very nice."

The water was only up to her waist now, and his eyes swept over her body. Here it comes. Kelly braced herself. He was surely going to kiss her now. But T. just smiled and dove back out into the deeper water.

She had been so positive he was going to kiss her, *so* sure. She had actually started feeling relieved that today's waiting was over. But then he went and didn't do it, damn him. He was driving her crazy, and she couldn't stand the uncertainty another minute longer. "Tyrone Jackson, get your butt back here."

"Uh-oh," he said as he swam back toward her. "What'd I do now?"

"Kiss me. Will you just kiss me, damn it, and get it over with?"

He stood up then, and water fell off his body in a sheet. Two big steps brought him right to her side, close enough to put his arms around her, close enough for her to see that the swirl of color in his eyes matched the sunlit ocean almost exactly. She swallowed and looked away, unable to hold the intensity of his gaze.

"Do you want me to?" he asked softly.

"No!" T. started to turn away. If he didn't kiss her now, she'd spend the entire day on edge— "Yes, okay? *Yes!*"

He looked at her and it wasn't the sizzling look of desire she had expected. Instead, he smiled rather wistfully. But he still didn't kiss her.

"Please, T.," she whispered.

He touched her then, one hand lightly brushing her hair back from her face, his eyes soft. "Aw, Kel," he breathed. "I didn't want to use up today's kiss right now, but you know I can't refuse you anything."

He leaned forward and his lips brushed against hers, gently at first, then with increasing pressure.

Kelly felt his arms go around her, his hands on her bare back, pressing her against him. It was as if the sensation of their two wet, nearly naked bodies was too much for Jackson, because he didn't end the kiss when she expected him to. He just kept kissing her, harder, deeper now. Of course, maybe it had something to do with the fact that her arms were up around his neck, and that she was kissing him as hungrily as he was kissing her.

She wanted him. She couldn't deny it any longer. She was ready to surrender, ready to stop pretending that she didn't lie awake all night, wishing that she were in T.'s bed.

"Kelly, I love you so much," T. said, kissing her face. "I need you."

She could feel his heart pounding, hear the raggedness of each breath as his mouth found hers again.

He pulled her out with him, deeper, and under the private cover of the water, he touched her, cupping the softness of her breasts, caressing, stroking. Kissing her hard, harder, he pressed against her. There was no mistaking what he wanted.

And, quite clearly, Kelly knew that making love with T. Jackson was what she wanted, too.

But suddenly he tore himself away, backing off about five feet. He just stood there, breathing hard and looking at her. His eyes seemed luminous, and Kelly realized it was unshed tears that made them shine.

Before she could say a word, he turned and dove into the water. He surfaced far down the beach and kept swimming, hard, away from her.

"T., come back," Kelly whispered, but there was no way on earth he could have heard.

By dinnertime Kelly convinced herself that her moment of surrender when T. had kissed her in the water had been merely that. A moment.

She had been temporarily insane, momentarily crazed. Hadn't she?

Of course, the fact that T. Jackson hadn't returned from the beach until she was in the shower helped her regain her misplaced sanity. By the time she was done, he had vanished, taking his car with him. He hadn't left a note saying where he'd gone and when he'd be back.

It was definitely much easier to convince herself that she didn't want him when he wasn't around.

She worked all day, pretending she wasn't wondering where he was as she rewrote that damned love scene.

It wasn't until six o'clock, when the sun was sinking in the sky, that Jackson appeared.

"How's it going?" He set cartons of Chinese food on the big conference table, along with several plates he'd brought from the kitchen.

He was still wearing his green bathing suit, though it had long since dried. His hair was a mess, but it only made him look even more charming than usual.

As Kelly met his eyes, she knew immediately that everything she'd been trying to tell herself about T. Jackson all afternoon had been a load of hogwash. If he as much as said a word, she'd throw herself into his arms.

"You getting that scene rewritten?" He opened a carton of steaming brown rice.

"I'm trying." Kelly had to clear her throat before the words came out.

"Want me to read what you've got?"

"I don't think so."

"You've got to let me read it sooner or later." T. flashed her a low-watt smile.

She stood and stretched, then sat down across from him at the table. "Later. Much later." She reached to open the third carton. It was unidentifiable, but it smelled great. Wow, she hadn't realized how hungry she was. She'd worked straight through lunch.

T. handed her a pair of paper-wrapped chopsticks, and they ate in silence.

Finally he cleared his throat. "Kel, I want to apologize for this morning."

She glanced at him, and his eyes were a very serious shade of green. But he couldn't hold her gaze, and he looked away.

"I went too far," he said quietly. "I'm sorry and I—"

"T.—"

"Please, let me finish, okay?"

He looked up at her, and she nodded slowly.

"I don't seem to have very much control when it comes to you. I'm afraid—" He cleared his throat again. "I'm afraid I'm not going to hear you or understand you when you tell me to stop, and I can't deal with the thought that I might—" He shook his head and took a deep breath. "Anyway, you don't have to worry, I'm not going to kiss you again."

It was then that Kelly knew with absolute certainty that she wanted him to kiss her again. Wanted? Hell, she *needed* him to kiss her.

She stood. "Let me get this straight. You're not going to kiss me again, because you don't want to make love to me."

Jax shook his head, laughing with frustration. "That's the problem. I *do* want to make love to you." He watched as she walked around the table and sat down in the chair next to his. "Desperately." He pushed his half-eaten dinner away from him. "You've read my letters, Kelly. You know how I feel. I love you. I'm just afraid—''

"That when I say no, you won't be able to stop,'' Kelly finished for him. "The message won't get through.''

"Yeah.'' Jax rubbed his forehead as if he had a headache. He stood suddenly. "I need a beer. You want a beer?''

She stood, too. "T., wait.''

Even with the windows open wide and the salty ocean breeze blowing into the room, Jax could smell Kelly's sweet scent. She was standing much too close. He tried to take a step backward, but bumped into the table. She moved even closer.

"Watch my mouth,'' Kelly said. "And listen really carefully.''

"Kel—''

"Come on, T.,'' she said. "Watch and listen.''

Jax couldn't find any answers in her eyes, so he dropped his gaze to her soft lips.

"Are you listening?'' she asked, and he nodded.

Her lips curved upward into an enchanting smile, and then she said, quite clearly, "No.''

Jax closed his eyes. Torture. She was torturing him.

"You have any trouble understanding that?''

Eyes still closed, he shook his head. "Of course not. But these are hardly the same conditions that—''

"Okay, then, kiss me,'' Kelly ordered him.

He opened his eyes. "What?''

She smiled at him again. "Put your arms around me and kiss me,'' she repeated. "Gee, I didn't think I'd have to ask you *twice*.''

"Kel—''

"Come on, Tyrone. *Kiss* me. I can't prove my point until you do."

"And which point is it that you're trying to prove?"

Kelly laughed. "Kiss me and you'll find out."

Forget torture. She was trying to kill him. "I'm not sure this is such a good idea." He looked down at her mouth, and it was his undoing. She was moistening her lips with the tip of her tongue, and, God, he *had* to kiss her.

She was standing close, but not close enough, and as his mouth went down to meet hers, he pulled her in toward him. Just as his lips brushed hers, she reached up and, pressing the palms of her hands against his chest, she pushed herself back, away from him.

He let go of her instantly.

Kelly laughed. "You seemed to understand that, too."

Jax closed his eyes and pressed the heel of his hand against the bridge of his nose. This was going to be one *hell* of a headache when it finally arrived. If he lived that long. When he opened his eyes, Kelly was still standing directly in front of him, smiling up at him.

"Understand what?" he asked wearily.

She reached out and pushed against his chest with the palm of her hand again. "That," she said. "You know what it means when I do that, right?"

"Yeah. It means stop, don't, no."

"Well, there you have it. Two perfectly understandable ways to say no—one verbal, one not."

She looked so pleased with herself. "I hate to break it to you," he said, "but if you've just made your point, you lost me somewhere."

"Well, actually, no," she told him. "I haven't made my point yet. In order for me to do that, you have to kiss me again."

Jax sat down tiredly on top of the table. "Kel—"

They were nearly the same height now, and Kelly stepped in between his legs and draped her arms around his neck. "I suppose *I* could always kiss *you*." Leaning forward slightly, she did.

Her lips were soft, and tasted so sweet. She pulled back slightly, looking into his eyes and smiling before she kissed him again.

Jax opened his mouth under the gentle pressure from her tongue. She was kissing him. Kelly was kissing *him*. He couldn't decide whether to laugh or cry, so he did neither. Instead, he put his arms around her, crushing her to him, devouring the sweetness of her mouth with his own.

Kelly laughed, arching her head back as he rained kisses down her neck. "The reason you didn't hear me say no this morning was because I didn't say it. And if you listen very closely, you still won't hear me say no."

Jax couldn't breathe. "And how about if I pick you up and carry you into my bedroom?" he asked. "Will you still not say no?"

"Maybe you should give it a try," Kelly answered huskily.

He swung her up into his arms.

T.'s bedroom was lit only by the evening sunset. Red and orange light streamed in through the windows, making the white walls seem warm and pink. He set her gently on his bed, and Kelly reached for him, pulling him down next to her. She kissed him and slid her hands up, underneath his T-shirt, glad she'd finally given in.

"Kelly, wait," he said. He was breathing hard, and she knew by the accelerated beat of his heart that he didn't really want to stop. But he caught her hands. "You know how much I want to make love to you." His face was serious as his eyes searched hers.

She nodded. "I want it, too."

"Do you?" A muscle flickered in his jaw as he clenched and unclenched his teeth. "Do you really want to make love? Or is this just going to be sex?"

Kelly tried to smile. "Can't we figure that out later?"

T. was trying to smile, too, but she could see the hurt in his eyes. "An evasive answer. You still won't admit that you love me, will you?"

"Jackson—" Kelly looked down at the floor "—I'm just not ready—"

"For this," he finished with her. "I know."

He was still holding her hands, and he laced her fingers with his, squeezing them gently. "This might come as a shock to you, and God knows it's one hell of a shock to *me,* but I'm not going to settle for sex. I'm not going to settle, period. When you decide to admit to yourself that you love me, then I'll make love to you. But not until then." He drew her hands to his mouth and kissed them before he released her.

Kelly *was* shocked. She was shocked that he would actually turn her down, but mostly shocked at how disappointed she felt. "Well." Her voice sounded breathless and odd. "Who would've guessed that you'd end up being the one to say no?"

But T. shook his head vehemently. "I'm saying yes," he said. "To the question that really matters, Kel, I'm the one saying yes."

Chapter 14

Three o'clock in the morning, and Jax still sat in front of the computer, staring sightlessly at the screen. God, would this night never end?

He couldn't sleep. He'd tried that already, and all he did was lie in bed and think about the fact that Kelly wasn't there with him.

She should've been, and worst of all, she *could've* been. He'd lost his mind. That had to be the answer. No red-blooded, *hot*-blooded American man in his right mind would've turned down a woman like Kelly the way he had. He had suddenly been possessed by the spirit of these damned romantic heroes he obviously spent too much time writing about.

"So go and tell her you were wrong," a familiar voice cut through his thoughts. Jared was sitting on a bed in one of the guest rooms of the sprawling ranch house. He looked dashing, as usual, his thick, glossy hair disheveled and his shirt off. His arm was still bleeding. The bullet had gone clear through, and Carrie was bandaging both sides of the wound. "Tell Kelly," Jared said, "that you were temporarily insane and that you'll gladly settle for a pure, uncomplicated sexual relationship— Ouch!"

He looked up at Carrie in surprise as she was none too gentle with his arm. "He *loves* her," Carrie said to Jared. "Has it occurred to you that he might actually want more than just a sexual relationship? And I don't care what you say, *no* relationship is *ever* uncomplicated."

"Look, guys," Jax broke in. "We're coming up on the ending to this story here. Could we maybe be a little nicer to each—"

"*I'm* being incredibly nice," Jared declared. "Man, she *shot* me, and I'm still offering to stick around and help her defend her ranch and her water rights against those outlaws—"

"I don't want or need your help," Carrie said tightly. "As soon as I'm done wrapping you up, I will thank you very much to take your oversize horse and your oversize ego off of my land."

"Hang on!" Jax said. "Let me get some of this on disk." He started to write.

"You need help," Jared said bluntly. "Who're you gonna get it from? That old man you got working in your stables? Or maybe that little boy I saw running across the yard a minute ago?"

"Well, at least I know they won't desert me."

"Whoa now," Jared said, catching her arm before she could turn away. "I never deserted you. I *told* you I would come back for you. You didn't wait for me!"

"I couldn't wait."

"You didn't want to wait," he accused her.

Carrie laughed, but there was no humor on her pretty face. "No, Jared, I *couldn't*. I was carrying your child."

Shock. Complete numbing shock. A…*child?*

"We have a child?" Jared breathed.

"A son."

Outside the window, across the yard, the little boy was helping the old man brush down Jared's stallion. Slowly Jared pulled himself to his feet, crossing to the window, staring out at…his son?

Jared turned to her. "Carrie, God, I didn't know."

It had been purely by accident that he had deserted Carrie more than eight years ago. If he had known she needed him so desperately, he would've walked through hell to get to her.

Now she was in trouble again, and he was damned if he was going to desert her a second time.

Kelly couldn't sleep. She sat on her bed, looking at the pile of letters T. Jackson had written to her in the few weeks she'd been here.

He loved her.

There was proof of that in these letters. As if she'd really need any other proof after tonight… T. never would've refused a chance to go to bed with her if he didn't love her.

She felt tears welling up in her eyes. She couldn't let herself love him back. It would hurt too much when he stopped loving her. And he *would* stop loving her. Or maybe he just wouldn't love her enough to stick around. He'd loved her seven years ago, but not enough to fight for her, not even enough to come back for her when she turned eighteen the way he'd promised.

No, she couldn't risk letting herself love him.

The best thing for both of them was for Kelly to pack her things and go back to Boston.

She wiped her eyes on the sleeve of her T-shirt and took her suitcase out of the closet. It didn't take her long to pack her clothes, but the sun was starting to peek over the edge of the horizon by the time she was done.

One more walk on the beach. She'd take one more walk before she woke up Jackson to ask him to drive her to the bus station.

The dawn air was damp, but the sun was already hot enough to start burning off the mist and ocean fog. The beach was deserted and quiet, with only the sounds of the water and the seagulls breaking the calm.

In just a few hours, she'd be back in Boston, back in the noisy city, away from the beach. Away from T.

She'd be alone again, working in the solitude of her apartment, unable to turn around and ask a stupid grammar question or share a joke, a comment, a smile.

Fact was, she was going to miss T. Jackson.

Kelly's bare toes dug into the wet sand as she walked, and she tried to brush away the tears that had gathered again in her eyes. She was going to miss more than T.'s keen sense of humor and his help editing her manuscript. She was going to miss the way his eyes crinkled up at the corners when he laughed. She was going to miss the fact that he could get dressed up to the nines for dinner in a hand-tailored suit and *still* not wear any socks. She was going to miss his teasing, his jokes, the way he smiled at her when he said "Good morning."

And she was going to miss his kisses.

Her tears were falling faster now, and Kelly just sat down in the sand at the edge of the water and cried.

Who was she trying to kid? She was in love with T. Jackson Winchester the Second. There was no doubt about it.

A romantic hero would stick to his guns and not give in.

But Jax wasn't any kind of romantic hero, and the fact remained that as much as he wanted Kelly to admit that she was in love with him, there was no guarantee that she was going to.

The fact also remained that after a long, sleepless night, Jax realized as much as it would hurt him in the long run, he was willing to take whatever Kelly was willing to give. And if that meant having a no-strings, no-commitment relationship based on a sexual attraction…well, at least there would be some pleasure with his pain.

When it came to Kelly, he was weak. He would be the first to admit that.

He stood outside Kelly's bedroom door. There was no sound from inside. Of course there wasn't. It wasn't even 6:00 a.m.

Jax knocked softly on the door, but there was no answer. He tried the knob, and it turned. The door was unlocked, so he pushed it open.

The room was empty; the bed hadn't even been slept in. And Kelly's suitcase was packed and standing in the middle of the floor.

She was going to leave.

Pain hit him hard and square in the middle of his chest, and he struggled to breathe. Kelly was going to leave.

He heard a sound, and turned to see her standing in the doorway. She looked so beautiful. Her hair was tousled from the wind and curling from the humidity. Her T-shirt was damp from the ocean's spray and it clung to her soft curves. Her cheeks were flushed, her eyes bright with tears—

Jax swallowed the last of his pride. "Kel, please don't go." His voice cracked slightly. He tried to smile. "You win. I'll play by your rules. We'll do this your way."

Kelly watched him rake his fingers through his thick blond hair. He wasn't trying to hide his desperation from her, and she could see it in his eyes, hear it in his voice.

"T.—" she started.

"You don't have to love me." He took a step forward. "I know that you care about me, and that's good enough for now."

He was making a sacrifice. He was willing to toss aside the things he wanted in order to keep her near him.

"No, T.—"

"Kelly, please." Another step, and he took her hands in his. His eyes were fiercely determined. "If you leave, I'm just going to follow you. I can't live without you. I don't want to live without you. I *refuse* to live without you—"

He kissed her, a hard, demanding, hungry kiss that sent fire racing through her blood. With his arms around her as he held her tightly to him, she could feel his heart beating as he whispered, "Please, don't go. I was wrong—"

"No, you were right." Kelly reached up to touch the side of his face and realized her hand was shaking. God, what she felt for this man scared her to death. She didn't want to say the words aloud. But she had to, if only to relieve the look of desperation in his eyes. "You've been right all along—"

"Right now there is no wrong or right," Jax said, shaking his head. "All I know is that I'd do damn near anything to make you stay."

She was in his arms, and he was looking down into the bottomless depths of her eyes. His memories of those eyes had been his savior, his connection to sanity, blurring the line between reality and fantasy during a time when reality would have broken him.

Now her eyes were filled with tears, tears that escaped to run down the exquisite softness of her cheeks.

"You don't have to," Kelly told him quietly, "because, God help me, I love you, T."

Did she just say that she loved him? He stared at her. Had her words been fantasy or reality?

"What did you say?" he whispered.

"I love you. God knows I don't want to, but I do."

Reality.

With a sudden blinding flash, Jax could see his future stretching out in front of him, and for the first time in ages, it was lit by sunshine and laughter. She loved him. Kelly had finally admitted that she loved him.

He kissed her, tasting the salt of her tears, the sweetness of her lips. He could see the love in her eyes. It wasn't new—he'd seen it there before—but she wasn't trying to hide or ignore it now.

"T., make love to me," Kelly said.

"Come to my room," he breathed, and she nodded.

Holding her hand, Jax led her down the hall to his bedroom, drawing her inside and locking the door behind her. He closed the door that led to his office, then turned to look at her.

Kelly stood in the center of the room, watching T. He looked exhausted, and she knew that, like her, he hadn't slept at all last night. But he smiled at her, a smile that erased the fatigue from his face and lit his eyes with happiness.

She realized she couldn't let herself think about the future. She couldn't think about the pain and heartache that would surely come from loving him. There would be plenty of time to suffer when he was gone. But right now he was here, and here and now were what mattered. Here and now his heart was hers.

Kelly smiled at him. "Can we take this from where we left it last night?" She crossed to the bed and sat on the edge. "I think I was over here."

T. walked across the room almost impossibly slowly, holding her gaze every step of the way. The fire from his eyes burned into her body, infusing her with a heat that seemed to rise from deep within her. As he sat down next to her on the bed, he picked up her hands, lacing their fingers together.

He kissed her, and Kelly could feel his restraint. He was holding back, as if he were afraid to overwhelm her, as if he were afraid he'd lose control.

"It's not many people who get a second chance to make love for the first time," he said with a crooked smile.

"I'm going to have to disappoint you," Kelly admitted. "That night in your hotel room? That wasn't just sex. We *were* making love. I loved you then—I was just too stupid to admit it.''

''I'm not disappointed.'' He kissed her again, still so carefully.

Kelly reached up, lightly tracing the small scar on his cheekbone as she looked into his eyes. Like the high school boy who had scarred him in that fight, she knew firsthand about the passion that burned inside of T. Jackson.

She loved T. because he was sweet and kind and funny and smart. But the fact that he could manage so successfully to hide his passion behind a cool and collected facade of control made her love him even more. Especially since she knew that she had the power to take that control of his and tear it to shreds.

Which was exactly what she intended to do right now.

She knelt next to him on the bed and kissed him fiercely, pulling him closer to her, running her hands up underneath his T-shirt, against his smooth, muscular back. She could feel his control slipping as his arms tightened around her, as he returned her kisses. Drawing her leg across him, she straddled his lap, and he groaned.

Together they pulled his T-shirt off, then hers, tossing them onto the floor. Her bra soon followed.

Picking Kelly up, Jax turned, pushing her back onto the bed, covering her body with his. ''I love you, Kel,'' he breathed, touching, caressing the smooth softness of her neck, her shoulders, her breasts.

As he kissed her again, his fingers fumbled with the button on her cutoff jeans. Nearly growling with frustration, he pulled away from her. Laughing, she unfastened the button, then, holding his gaze, slowly drew the zipper down.

As she slipped out of her shorts and her panties, Jax could barely breathe. He was frozen in place, spellbound, hypnotized. "Are you real?" he whispered. "Are you really here with me, or am I dreaming?"

For a long time after he'd returned from Central America, he had been struck by feelings of unreality, expecting at any moment he would awaken still locked in his prison cell. He felt that way now.

Kelly sat up, putting her arms around his neck as she kissed him. "If you think you're dreaming, maybe you better hurry up, get your clothes off and make love to me before you wake up."

Jax laughed, then gasped as her hands found the hardness of his arousal pressing against his shorts. She deftly undid the button and his shorts quickly followed the rest of their clothes onto the floor.

He quickly covered himself with a condom, then slipped between her legs. His hands and mouth were everywhere then, touching her, kissing her, drinking in the softness of her skin, the wet heat of her desire.

"Tell me again that you love me," he whispered, looking down into her eyes.

He was poised over her, the muscles in his arms and shoulders flexed as he kept his weight lifted off of her. His golden hair was a jumble of unruly waves, messed from her fingers.

She smiled up at him, and he kissed her again, as if he couldn't bear to be separated from her lips for too long.

"I love you," she said. "I always have."

He filled her then, both her heart and her body, and for the first time in her life, she felt truly whole. She had loved him forever, a love so pure and true, it had triumphed over the passage of time and all of her pain and heartache. She knew in that instant she would love him until the end of time, long after he'd moved on.

She held him close, moving with him, pushing him farther, more deeply inside of her, hoping if she held him tightly enough, he would never go away.

"I love you," she cried, the waves of her pleasure exploding through her.

She felt T.'s body tighten with his own stormy release, heard him call her name, his voice hoarse with passion.

Don't ever leave me, she thought.

It wasn't until T. answered her that she realized she had spoken the words aloud. "I won't, Kel," he said, kissing her sweetly. "I promise I won't."

But it was a promise he'd already broken once before.

Chapter 15

"Do you want to go for a swim or make love?" T. asked, nuzzling Kelly's neck.

The morning sun was streaming through the windows of his bedroom, and Kelly stretched. "What day is it?"

He smiled at her lazily. "I can only give you a rough estimate—I can tell you the month and the year. Well, wait a minute, maybe I can't even do that. Is it July or August? It could be August."

Kelly laughed. "Impossible. August was at least a week away. I mean, all you need is love and all that, but I just can't believe someone as spoiled as you—"

"Spoiled?" T. feigned insult.

"—could go for a whole week without food," Kelly finished teasingly.

But suddenly he wasn't laughing anymore. His eyes were strangely haunted and his smile disappeared. "You'd be surprised at how long I could go without food,'' he said quietly. But just as quickly as that odd mood had fallen over him, it was gone. He smiled with a quick flash of his white teeth and pulled her on top of him, kissing her hard on the mouth.

''I have a deadline coming up,'' he told her, ''and I'm having a bitch of a time finishing this book. Argh! I don't want to think about it. I don't even want to work on it anymore.'' He kissed her again, then looked thoughtful. ''Of course, if it *is* August, then I'm already late with the manuscript, and there're probably twenty-five very irate messages from my editor on my answering machine.''

''And if it's August, Stefanie and Emilio are back from their cruise,'' Kelly pointed out.

''Oh, damn, there goes our privacy.'' T. closed his eyes with pleasure as she ran her fingers through his hair. ''No more running naked through the house.''

''Have you been running naked through the house?'' Kelly teased. ''Without me?''

''Well, no.'' He caught her hands and kissed the tips of her fingers. ''But you know how it is. As soon as you can't do something, you immediately want to do it.''

''If I tell you that you absolutely *can't* work on your manuscript, will that make you want to finish writing it?''

''No. But I just got a sudden wild craving to play miniature golf.''

Kelly laughed.

''And then I want to call your parents and tell them that we're getting married.''

She froze. T. was smiling up at her. He hadn't shaved in days and his hair was wild, but with his eyes lit with love, he was so utterly handsome he took her breath away. But she wasn't going to marry him. She couldn't. "T., we're not getting married."

He was unperturbed. "Yes, we are."

"No, we're *not*. Besides, that's not the sort of thing you're supposed to just *tell* someone. You're supposed to *ask*— Didn't we have this conversation once before?"

He turned suddenly, flipping Kelly onto her back, pinning her to the bed with his body. "Marry me," he said, all teasing gone from his voice and eyes. "Kelly, please, will you marry me?"

As she looked up at him, her eyes filled with tears. "How many years do you want to marry me for, T.?" she asked. "Two? Maybe three?" She pushed him away from her and sat up on the edge of the bed. "I can't go through that again."

"I'm not Brad," Jax said quietly. "I want you for forever."

She turned to face him. "That's what Brad said, too. But he changed his mind."

"Maybe he realized that you didn't love him. Maybe he figured out that you were still in love with me."

Kelly just watched him quietly, and Jax wished he could get inside her head, read her mind and know what she was thinking.

"I love you," he said. "And you love me. We should have been together right from the very start—"

"If you believe that, then why did you go to London?"

It was a direct question, deserving of a point-blank answer. Jax looked straight into Kelly's eyes and fired both barrels.

"Because Kevin gave me a choice between going

to London or being brought up on charges of attempted rape."

Kelly was shocked. Attempted *rape?* "That's ridiculous—"

"You were underage." His eyes were intense as he tried to make her understand. "If Kevin had made any noise, there would've been an investigation at the very least. It would've been horrible, Kel, not just for me, but for you. You would've been examined by doctors, questioned by the police and all kinds of social workers and psychologists. And God, if any word at all had slipped out to the papers, it would've been a total media circus. Your reputation would have been shredded." He was silent, looking out the windows at the deep, clear blue of the sky. "I didn't give a damn about myself, but I couldn't do that to you, so I went to London."

"Kevin was bluffing!"

"I sure as hell didn't think so."

"Why didn't you at least talk to me about it?"

"It was part of the deal," Jax said. "I couldn't try to see you. I couldn't call. I couldn't even write to you."

"I thought you didn't love me," she said softly.

He shook his head. "It was because I loved you that I left. And if I had to do it over again, I'm not sure I wouldn't do exactly the same thing."

Kelly was older now, but he could still see that sweet sixteen-year-old girl when he looked into her eyes. He had let her down all those years ago.

"You broke my heart." It wasn't an accusation. It was a fact. And somehow that made it even worse.

"That part I'd do differently," Jax told her.

* * *

Jax sat at his computer, looking out his office windows. If he craned his neck, he could see down to the deck where Kelly was sitting, reading the unfinished draft of his manuscript. She was wearing the black bathing suit he'd bought her. Black bathing suit, black sunglasses, all that lightly tanned, smooth skin...

"Aren't you supposed to be writing?" Jared's familiar voice broke into his thoughts. "Look, Kelly's a real babe, but can't you take your eyes off of her for even a few minutes?"

Jax dragged his eyes back to the computer screen. He had left Jared out in the barn, brushing down his stallion. A light rain was falling outside of the open barn door.

"Kelly's finally mine." Jax laughed. "I am *so* lucky—"

"Yeah, well, she hasn't agreed to marry you, so don't send the tux out to the dry cleaners yet." Jared wiped the sweat from his brow with the sleeve of his cotton shirt. "You may have the 'happily' part down, but the 'ever after' needs some work."

"You're just jealous—" Jax crossed his arms and leaned back in his chair "—because Carrie still won't have anything to do with you."

"Yeah, well, she doesn't trust me," Jared admitted. "But hey, you know what they say about art imitating life."

Jax frowned, leaning forward. "Are you intimating that Kelly doesn't trust me?"

"That's exactly what I'm 'intimating.'" Jared grinned. "Man, where do you come up with these words?"

"I'm a writer," Jax said absently.

"Coulda fooled me," Jared said dryly. "I've been

hanging out, waiting for you to write me out of this barn for days.''

Jax was deep in thought. Kelly didn't trust him? Yeah, it made sense. "Is it men in general that she doesn't trust?" he wondered out loud. "Or is it me?"

"Mostly you," Jared guessed. "You hurt her badly once already. She's waiting for you to do it again."

"So what am I supposed to do?" Jax asked, adding, "God, I must be desperate if I'm reduced to asking *you* for advice."

Jared leaned against the doorframe, crossing his arms in front of him. Thinking hard, he looked down at the toes of his dusty boots as he scuffed them in the dirt. When he looked back at Jax, there was a twinkle in his dark eyes.

"Maybe you should let life imitate art for a change," he said with a smile. "How do you plan to get Carrie to agree to marry *me?* Just do the same thing with Kelly."

Jax ran his fingers through his hair and laughed, a short, humorless burst of air. "It's hardly the same situation—"

"It's *exactly* the same—"

"If you must know, you're going to take a bullet that was meant for Carrie," Jax told his character. "When you nearly die, she's going to realize how much you mean to her."

"You're going to have me get shot *again?*" Jared straightened up. "That's one gunshot wound for every...what? Every hundred and ten pages? Thank the Lord this book's only four hundred and fifty pages long. I'm beginning to feel like I'm walking around with a sign around my neck saying 'Shoot me, I'm a romantic hero.'"

"Stop complaining," Jax said, tipping his chair back on two legs. "It's going to get you what you want, *and* you're going to save Carrie's life."

"Just watch your aim, okay?" Jared began to pace. His big horse snorted and glanced back over his shoulder at him. "Well, obviously you can't use that same solution for your problem."

"Obviously."

"Ahem."

Jax lost his balance and his chair went over backward with a crash. "Hi." He smiled weakly up at Kelly from the floor.

In the barn, Jared was laughing.

"You really do talk to yourself, don't you?" She put the notebook that held his manuscript down on the table.

She'd put a big, filmy gauze blouse on over her bathing suit. The tails came down to her knees, but she'd left the front unbuttoned. The flashes of smooth, tanned skin that Jax could see beneath the white gauze made his mouth go dry.

She held out her hand to help him up, but instead of getting to his feet, he pulled her down onto the floor with him.

"I wasn't talking to myself," he said, kissing her. "I was talking to Jared."

"Jared." She nodded. "You outdid yourself with him. He's a real hunk, and I mean to-die-for in a major way. I think he's your best hero yet."

"Oh, yeah!" Jared strutted across the barn. "She likes me. Watch out, Winchester, you're history."

"Yeah, well, you're fictional," Jax countered. Kelly was looking at him, one eyebrow raised, and he kissed her quickly. "Sorry. Just...you know..." He cleared his throat. "So you liked Jared, huh? And how about Kelly— *Carrie*," he corrected himself, then rolled his eyes.

Kelly laughed. "Ah, the truth comes out with the old Freudian slip. I *thought* she looked suspiciously like me. Well, a glorified, perfect me, anyway. And Jared's obviously you, only not blond and a little bit more stupid."

"Hey!" Jared was insulted.

"More stupid!" Jax repeated happily. "That's a great way to describe him. I like it. More stupid. I can picture the blurb on the back cover now. 'Jared Dexter, stronger and braver than most, more stupid than some—'"

"Oh, shut up." Jared turned his back pointedly, picking up the brush and starting in on his horse's coat again.

Laughing, Jax kissed Kelly. "He's pouting now."

"If you told me you planned to shoot me, I'd pout, too," Kelly said, pulling herself to her feet.

"How long were you listening to me—"

"Talk to yourself?" Kelly finished for him with a grin. "Long enough to know that you're planning to get Carrie and Jared together with the old hero-almost-dies ploy. It's been used before, but that's okay."

She was standing with her back to the windows, and the sunlight streamed in behind her, making her cover-up seem to disappear. "There's just one thing I need to ask you."

Jax held up one hand. "Wait. Let me get rid of some distractions." He cleared the computer screen, then walking toward her, he took her gently by the arm and switched their positions, so that he had his back to the window. From where he stood now, the sunlight streaming in made her shirt opaque again. "Okay, now I'm listening."

"Why hasn't Jared told Carrie where he was all those years?" Kelly asked. "I mean, my God, he went through hell, and Carrie doesn't have a clue. As far as she's concerned, he *did* desert her. Why doesn't he say something?"

Jax frowned down at the floor. This was it. He had to tell her. As much as he didn't want to, he knew he had to. It was definitely time.

Kelly leaned back against the table, waiting for his reply. As she watched, T. moistened his lips and cleared his throat. When he finally looked up at her, he had the strangest expression on his face.

"What's he gonna say?" he asked her quietly. "How's he going to bring it up? It's not easy for him to talk about, you know, what he went through. And it's sure as hell not a topic of conversation to have over dinner. He can't just say, 'Oh, by the way, I spent twenty godforsaken months of my life in a rat-infested prison in Central America.'"

Kelly frowned. What? Wait a minute, Jared hadn't been anywhere near Central America and...

"How *do* you tell someone something like that?" T.'s voice sounded oddly tight. "Do you just walk up and say, 'Sorry I missed your eighteenth birthday, but I was a political prisoner in a country where the phrase "human rights" isn't in the dictionary?' How do you tell someone you love that you were locked in a four-by-eight room, given barely enough food and water to stay alive for nearly two years?"

"Oh my God," she breathed. He wasn't talking about Jared. He was talking about...*himself!*

With a sudden flash of memory, she saw T. as he

was at Kevin's wedding, thin to the point of gauntness, as if he'd been ill or…nearly starved to death. She heard an echo of Stefanie's shocked voice, from the day they'd had lunch together. *He never told you what happened in Central America?*

Kelly felt sick.

"What's he going to say to her?" T. said again. He turned away and looked out the window at the sunlight dancing across the water.

Heart pounding, Kelly crossed toward him. As she put her arms around his waist, he looked down at her and forced a smile. "It's just not easy to talk about."

"What if she asks?" she said softly. "Will he tell her then?"

"Yeah."

"T., tell me about…Central America?"

He closed his eyes and drew a deep breath, then slowly let it out before turning and looking out at the water again.

"I went there for an interview with an opposition leader," T. said. He was trying to sound normal, as if they were talking about last night's Red Sox game instead of his…incarceration. Oh, God. Kelly could see tears in his eyes, but he staunchly ignored them, managing to look only slightly less cool and collected than he usually did. "After I talked to him, the government thought I might have information on the whereabouts of the rebel forces. They failed to, um, persuade me to part with any of my information—of which I had very little—and on my way to the airport, I was arrested. Someone had planted a small fortune in cocaine in my overnight bag. I was sentenced to ten years in prison. I was really a political prisoner, but the American consulate couldn't do anything to help me, because of the drug charges.''

Tears escaped from his eyes, and he brushed them brusquely away. ''I'm sorry,'' he said quickly.

Kelly punched him, and he looked at her in surprise.

''Don't you *dare* apologize,'' she said hotly. ''My God, I can't even imagine how terrible it must have been. Jackson, how can you stand there like that and give me the impersonal Journalism 101 synopsis?''

''I'm sorry—''

''*Stop* apologizing!'' she shouted. ''You should be furious, angry, *outraged* that this happened to you. God, T., did they hurt you? Did you cry? Were you alone? What did you do? Did they make you work? Tell me what it smelled like. Tell me how you found the strength to survive! Tell me how you *felt!*''

Kelly paced back and forth, nearly shaking her fist in the air. She whirled to face him. ''*Show* me how you felt, damn it. Get pissed! Throw something! Break some furniture—''

''I love you,'' Jax said. ''And you love me. That's all I need to feel now, Kelly.'' He pulled her into his arms. ''I can show you that, and I will—every day for the rest of our lives, if you'll let me.''

She was crying, hot, angry tears, and Jax gently caught one with his finger. ''Besides—'' he smiled slightly and kissed her ''—I don't break furniture. I write.''

He pulled away from her and crossed to his big bookshelf. Reaching up, he took a heavy blue three-ring binder down from among all the other notebooks and handed it to her. ''This will tell you how I felt.''

Kelly looked down at the manuscript as she wiped the tears from her face. ''A story?''

"Nonfiction," T. told her. "Although, when I publish it, I should probably give cowriting credit to my psychologist. I'd meant to get this all down on paper when I first came back, but it was my shrink who finally forced me to sit down and write it."

He kissed her again. "I'll be on the beach," he said, but she'd already sat down at the table, opening up the thick manuscript to the first page. She didn't even hear him as he slipped out the door.

It was called *Letters to Kelly,* she realized with shock. Leafing quickly through, she saw that the entire manuscript was a series of letters—all addressed to her. Heart pounding, she began to read.

After the first few pages, she was in tears again.

Dear Kelly,
I regain consciousness in my cell, and I am surprised—surprised that I am still alive. I'm lucky. I saw the bodies of less fortunate men being dumped into the back of a pickup truck the last time I was in the courtyard.

But then I move, and my entire body screams with pain. And I wonder. Maybe *they* were the lucky ones....

Dear Kelly,
Four days since I've last been fed. You come and keep me company, and we talk about Thanksgiving dinner. You take my hand and pull me back with you, back in time, and I'm at your house. Your dining room table has been extended, and your parents and your grandmother, your aunt Christa and your cousins, Kevin, you and I all sit, bowing our heads as your father says grace.

I stare at the feast on the table, realizing that the leftovers from this meal could keep me alive for months....

Outside the office window, the sun moved across the sky, but Kelly was aware of nothing but the words on the paper. T.'s words. Letters he'd written her, from hell.

T. Jackson was sitting on the beach, arms wrapped loosely around his knees, watching the sunset. The wind ruffled his golden blond hair, and the sunlight flashed as it hit the reflective lenses of his sunglasses. He had a bottle of beer in his hand—he was a living advertisement for the good life.

He looked at Kelly as she sat down next to him. She knew what she looked like—her eyes were puffy and the tip of her nose was red. He put his arms around her and kissed the top of her head. "You all right?" he asked quietly.

"Shouldn't I be asking *you* that question?" Kelly reached up and took off his sunglasses so that she could see his eyes. They were beautiful, greenish-blue in the late-afternoon light, and so warm and loving.

"I'm extremely all right." He touched her hair and kissed her mouth. "In fact, I keep wondering if maybe I haven't actually died and gone to heaven. We're finally together, and you love me, too—"

Kelly started to cry, pressing her face into the warmth of his neck, holding him as tightly as she could.

"Hey," he said. "Hey, come on—"

"I'm sorry." Sobs shook her body. "Oh, T., I'm

so sorry. You came back from that...that...*place,* and I wasn't there for you."

"Kel—"

"All this time I thought you had deserted me, but *I* was the one who deserted you. All that time you were in that horrible prison and I didn't even try to find you—"

"It's okay, Kel." His voice was gentle, soothing. "You didn't know."

"T., I wasn't there for you."

"You're here for me now."

Kelly looked up at him, tears running down her face. "Yes, I am," she said, and she kissed him.

"You know, I meant it when I said that I won't ever leave you," he told her.

He had never stopped loving her. He would never stop loving her. Kelly believed that now. "I know."

T. smiled at her then, and wiping her eyes on the sleeve of her shirt, she managed to smile back at him. It was shaky, but it was definitely a smile.

"So," she said. "You want to go play a few rounds of miniature golf?" She laughed weakly at the surprised look on his face. "Or do you want to skip the golf and just call my parents and tell them that we're getting married?"

T. stared at her, his eyes opened wide, for several long seconds. Then he started to laugh. He kissed Kelly hard on the mouth, then jumped up and started dancing down the beach, whooping and shouting.

Kelly stared at him in shock, her mouth open. T. was acting so utterly uncool. She started to laugh. She loved it.

He froze suddenly, looking back at her.

"Are we really getting married?" he asked, as if he were making a quick reality check.

Kelly nodded. "I take it you still want to?"

He grabbed her hands and pulled her to her feet. "Oh, yeah." He kissed her, a deep, fiery kiss that left her dizzy. He swung her effortlessly up into his arms. His long legs covered the ground quickly as he carried her back toward the house. "This is definitely the best day of my life," he said, taking the stairs to the deck two at a time.

Jax opened the screen door into the living room and carried Kelly inside. He set her gently down, but her arms stayed around his neck and she kissed him. He groaned, opening his mouth under the pressure from her lips, sliding his hands underneath her big gauze shirt. Her skin was so soft and warm. He kissed her harder, deeper, shifting his hips so that she could feel his desire against her. She slid one smooth leg up, twisting it around his own leg, and breathing hard, he reached for the string that would untie the top of her bathing suit—

"Well, well, you two have certainly been busy since I've been gone," Stefanie's well-polished voice cut through.

Startled, Kelly sprang away from Jax, blushing and clutching her overshirt together.

"Stef," Jax said. "On your way in or out? Hopefully out."

She was in the entryway, a small suitcase in her hand. She laughed, amusement in her gray eyes. "Gee, what a welcome home. But no, lucky you, I'm going away for another month or so. Emilio's waiting in the car. We're flying to Italy to meet his parents." She rolled her eyes. "I've totally lost my mind. I've agreed to marry the man."

"Congratulations," Kelly said.

"Maybe we can make it a double wedding." Jax pulled Kelly in close to him, kissing the side of her face.

Stefanie's eyes softened. "Oh, darling, I'm so happy for you."

She looked at Kelly. "Thank God you finally came to your senses. I was ready to wring your little neck."

Kelly laughed. "I'm glad you didn't have to."

"Our flight leaves Boston in just a few hours." Stef's hand was on the doorknob. "I've got to run, but I *am* very glad." She waved to them. "See you when I see you, darlings."

The door closed with a bang behind her, leaving T. Jackson and Kelly staring at each other in the sudden stillness.

T. smiled, a slow, sexy smile that made Kelly's heart race. "Where were we before we were so rudely interrupted?" he asked.

She smiled. "I think we were about to run naked through the house."

"No, we've got a whole extra month to do that," he murmured, kissing the delicate skin under Kelly's ear. "We don't need to do that right now."

She closed her eyes, humming her approval of the placement of his lips and hands. "Maybe you wanted to go upstairs and finish writing your novel?"

"No, no, not the novel," he said. "But there was definitely something I wanted to do upstairs."

He took her hand and led her up to the second-floor landing.

"Maybe you wanted to write me another love letter."

At the top of the stairs he stopped and kissed her again and she melted against him.

"Haven't you read enough for today?" He lifted her up and carried her the last few steps into his bedroom.

"There's no such thing as too many love letters," Kelly pointed out.

He placed her gently on his bed, softly kissing her lips.

"Dear Kelly," he said, gazing into the depths of her eyes. "Let's skip the miniature golf, and call your parents much, *much* later—"

"Tomorrow," Kelly suggested, pulling his lips toward hers.

Tomorrow. Jax liked the sound of the word. Tomorrow, and the next day, and the next tomorrow after that, sliding way out into the infinite future, he'd have Kelly by his side. It was the only future he'd ever wanted, and it was finally his.

"Tomorrow sounds perfect," he breathed. "I love you. Love, T."

* * * * *

*Look out for more from Suzanne Brockmann
with* Scenes of Passion, *in June 2004
from Silhouette Desire.*

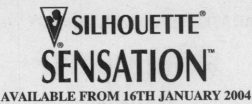

SILHOUETTE®
SENSATION™

AVAILABLE FROM 16TH JANUARY 2004

ONE OF THESE NIGHTS Justine Davis

Redstone, Incorporated

Ian Gamble couldn't believe it when he discovered his beautiful new neighbour, Samantha Beckett, was his bodyguard! But perhaps they should take her job description more *literally*?

MOMENT OF TRUTH Maggie Price

The Country Club

Police bomb technician Hart O'Brien had never expected to still feel a burning passion for first love Joan Cooper. But how would Hart react when he discovered Joan's ten-year-old secret?

BENEATH THE SILK Wendy Rosnau

Implicated in a murder, Sunni Blais needed help. But how could it come from the gorgeous man who'd been following her all week? And what would he do with her once he had her?

PRIVATE MANOEUVRES Catherine Mann

Wingmen Warriors

Undercover agent Max Keagan didn't need pilot Darcy Renshaw blowing his cover and getting them both killed. But while protecting Darcy, Max discovered he was in danger of losing his heart.

THE QUIET STORM RaeAnne Thayne

Detective Beau Riley knew heiress Elizabeth Quinn needed his help to protect a little boy. Beau's head was telling him to steer clear…but his heart was giving him a different message.

HONKY-TONK CINDERELLA Karen Templeton

After one night of passion Prince Aleksander Vlastos had left Luanne Evans with child and had regretted it ever since. Now Aleksander was determined to win a place back in their lives…

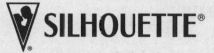

4 FREE

books and a surprise gift!

We would like to take this opportunity to thank you for reading this Silhouette® book by offering you the chance to take FOUR more specially selected titles from the Sensation™ series absolutely FREE! We're also making this offer to introduce you to the benefits of the Reader Service™—

- ★ FREE home delivery
- ★ FREE gifts and competitions
- ★ FREE monthly Newsletter
- ★ Exclusive Reader Service offers
- ★ Books available before they're in the shops

Accepting these FREE books and gift places you under no obligation to buy, you may cancel at any time, even after receiving your free shipment. Simply complete your details below and return the entire page to the address below. *You don't even need a stamp!*

YES! Please send me 4 free Sensation books and a surprise gift. I understand that unless you hear from me, I will receive 6 superb new titles every month for just £2.90 each, postage and packing free. I am under no obligation to purchase any books and may cancel my subscription at any time. The free books and gift will be mine to keep in any case.

S4ZED

Ms/Mrs/Miss/Mr ....Initials.....................................
                                                        BLOCK CAPITALS PLEASE

Surname ....

Address ....

....

....Postcode....................................

Send this whole page to:
UK: FREEPOST CN81, Croydon, CR9 3WZ
EIRE: PO Box 4546, Kilcock, County Kildare (stamp required)